"You want to kiss me, don't you?"

"I..." Shane's blood pounded. "Yes."

Zoe wet her lips. "Then you shouldn't have lied."

He reared back. "What are you talking about? I said yes. I wanted to kiss you. I always have."

"I meant that you lied about the lust potion. I know you analyzed it."

"Oh, that." She brought it up *now?*

She held his gaze, her lips curved into an inscrutable Mona Lisa smile. While he had no idea what she thought of him, there was a distinct likelihood that she knew *everything* that was in his mind, fantasies and all.

"I gather it's not looking good for my sample?" Zoe said.

"Probably not. I'm pretty sure it's a sham. Sorry to disappoint you."

Zoe turned to leave, but she stopped with one hand on the doorknob. "What I want to know," she said, "is that if the lust potion *doesn't* work, how come I'm so hot for you now, when I wasn't before?"

Blaze™

Dear Reader,

Some books are serendipitous. Even better when the magic happens with a trilogy!

The conception, brainstorming and writing of the LUST POTION #9 books was a breeze. Picture three authors in a convertible, laughing and gabbing, the wind in their hair. The brilliant and vivacious Colleen Collins, who originated the idea, is at the wheel. That's why we're speeding. The beautiful and funny Jamie Sobrato is riding shotgun. That's why we're getting whistled at. I'm in the back, giving directions off the map until it's whipped from my hands. That's why we're flying by the seat of our pants, free as birds but confident that we'll arrive in fine style.

I hope you've followed the lust potion through Jamie's *A Whisper of Wanting* and Colleen's *A Scent of Seduction*. And that you find the journey's end, *A Taste of Temptation*, worth the ride. To visit me online, go to www.CarrieAlexander.com and get connected to my group authors' blog, the Deadline Hellions.

All my best,

Carrie Alexander

A TASTE OF TEMPTATION
Carrie Alexander

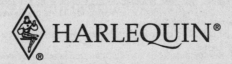

TORONTO • NEW YORK • LONDON
AMSTERDAM • PARIS • SYDNEY • HAMBURG
STOCKHOLM • ATHENS • TOKYO • MILAN • MADRID
PRAGUE • WARSAW • BUDAPEST • AUCKLAND

ISBN-13: 978-0-373-79300-6
ISBN-10:   0-373-79300-6

A TASTE OF TEMPTATION

Copyright © 2006 by Carrie Antilla.

www.eHarlequin.com

Printed in U.S.A.

ABOUT THE AUTHOR

Carrie Alexander has lost count of how many books she's written, but it's around thirty. Along the way, she's twice been a RITA® Award finalist and was recognized for career achievement from *Romantic Times BOOKreviews*. A lifelong Michigander, she's currently remaking a storybook cottage down by the river, where she paints anything that doesn't walk away. Which explains the lime-green garbage can and floral mailbox.

Books by Carrie Alexander
HARLEQUIN BLAZE
147—TASTE ME
163—UNWRAPPED
174—SLOW RIDE
236—HIDDEN GEMS

To Coco and Jamie
Goddesses of the Lust Potion

1

WHILE THE NEWSROOM BUZZED, clattered and even swirled around her, Zoe Aberdeen sat at her desk with her head in her hands. Her chin was three inches above the oversize calendar blotter she used as backup to her BlackBerry and spiral-bound notebook. If she didn't pull herself together, she'd drool on December ninth, where she'd written *Caballero y Salsa @ La Casa* in red marker. With two exclamation points.

"Need some hair of the dog?" asked a sympathetic British voice from behind her.

Zoe didn't swivel. Even shaking her head was too daunting to attempt. Her pickled brain would slosh around in her skull like the jar of dills that had sat at the back of her fridge for two years, ever since she'd settled in San Diego.

"Mmmph." She sucked her lower lip. "Got champagne?"

"There's no sense checking the kitchen. We only have hazelnut creamer and Red Bull." The rasp of Ethan Ramsey rubbing his jaw magnified to sandpaper on wood in Zoe's ears. "I can try to get a mimosa from Zanzibar."

"Good luck," Zoe mumbled. The local bar and grill delivered, but not alcohol and not so early in the day.

"Drinking on the job will get you fired," said another familiar voice. A concerned Kathryn Walters peeked over the edge of one of the cork-lined partitions that enclosed the colorfully decorated cubicle. At five eleven, she didn't have to stand on her toes to do it.

Zoe squinted to lessen the riotous glare of her dance club invitations, glitter-encrusted fairy wand and pink straw cowboy hat. "Never mind that drinking *is* my job."

She exaggerated. A major component of her work as a gossip columnist for the *San Diego Times* was to attend every club opening, charity ball and yacht launching that floated down the pipe. Despite her reputation as the *Times* columnist most likely to dance on tabletops, she tried to be mindful of overimbibing at the affairs she attended in a professional capacity. Even when she was off the clock and out with her friends, her high spirits didn't come from alcohol. Not completely.

The past night had been something else altogether....

"Where were you last night?" Kathryn asked.

"A *very* select holiday benefit for the symphony. They decorated with gold-leaf branches and twinkle lights and served the most expensive, delicious champagne I've ever tasted. But the evening was so dull, I—" Zoe stopped and swallowed the sour taste in her mouth. After she'd made notes about the chichi guest list and the dazzling decor, she'd had nothing left to do at the zero-exclamation-point-worthy soiree. Other than fend off questions from a pair of transplanted Bostonians who had known Zoe's family when they were prominent, accomplished and alive.

She pried her tongue off the roof of her mouth. "I overindulged."

"Clearly." Kathryn's voice was crisp.

"I can get you a headache remedy," Ethan said as he stepped into the cubicle. He was the *Times'* top crime reporter, a raffish Englishman who hadn't lost his taste for Inspector Dalgliesh and MI-5 despite an intense working knowledge of the somewhat less urbane San Diego legal and penal systems.

"Thanks, but I already popped a couple of pills." Zoe wagged a finger toward the variety of cure-alls she kept at hand in a brandy snifter on her desk. M&M's and breath mints mixed with one-dose packets of ibuprofen and NoDoz.

Kathryn sent a look toward Ethan. "What kind of pills?"

Zoe's eyeballs rolled. Luckily they kept to their sockets. "Strictly over-the-counter, if that's what you're thinking."

Kathryn's reputation was as arrow-straight as Zoe's was loosey-goosey. That is, until the buttoned-up book editor had reviewed an erotic thriller, fiddled with a counterfeit lust potion and gained the attention—to say the least—of Coyote Sullivan, a former coworker so overtly and indecently sexy that he could unsnap women's bras with merely a look.

Zoe's smile made her head wobble. Coyote was almost worth wearing a bra for. Lucky Kathryn.

"Steady on, Zoe," Ethan said. "Keep your profile low for the next few hours. Barbie—" Barbara Bitterman, their managing editor "—is on the warpath, looking for chinks in the staff's armor."

"If you can hold out, we'll treat you to lunch," offered Kathryn. "Food will help."

"Lunch seems a lifetime away." Zoe took a deep breath. With an effort, she shifted her head, balancing it very carefully until the room stopped whirling.

"But I will survive," she added, wincing inside at the retro familiarity of the phrase. She'd been to too many discos and experienced too much loss for one lifetime. Barbara Bitterman was only a mosquito of annoyance in the dark, tangled jungle of Zoe's psyche.

Nine years ago, Zoe's parents and older brother had been killed in a car accident on the way to her college graduation ceremony. She'd been twenty, on the verge of becoming a newly minted magna cum laude with a master's degree in comparative literature, destined to fulfill her Aberdeen destiny. At the funeral, she'd been told by an endless stream of intellectuals and potentates that she must survive—and thrive—to carry on the esteemed family name.

Afterward, when the shock wore off, Zoe had realized that she no longer wished to live a life of duty and boredom. Instead she'd abandoned the education that had meant so much to her parents, seized control of her trust fund and struck out on a series of desperately madcap jet-set adventures heretofore unknown to the stodgy, intellectual, old-money Aberdeen clan.

"Of course you'll survive," Kathryn soothed.

Zoe plastered on a carefree smile. "Yep. If I can live through a surfeit of yacht parties in Ibiza, ski trips to Aspen and Christmas holidays at a Thai beach resort, I can make it through one measly hangover."

Ethan chucked her under the chin. "You've had it real tough, kid."

Zoe kept up the smile. Her grief over her family had faded, or perhaps been buried under the glittering lie of her new lifestyle. Eventually the Aberdeen funds had slowed to a trickle. She'd been a spendthrift, and her "trustworthy" accountant had been overly liberal with his fees. The result was that she'd suddenly reached a point where it was either go broke or stop and take stock of her situation.

She took stock. Not a pretty sight.

Working her family connections and party-girl past, she'd landed the job at the *Times,* only to realize that she'd locked herself into a role she'd already been playing for too long. Fortunately she was good at it, even without the old trappings. Only Kathryn and a few close friends had an inkling that there was more to Zoe than her bright, flashy surface…and far less to her trust fund.

Today Zoe couldn't keep up the facade. She put her head in her hands. "I ran across old family friends at the symphony benefit. We, uh, caught up over champagne."

In fact, it had been the prospect of admitting to the couple that she'd spent the years since the elder Aberdeens' deaths traveling, partying and running through the family money like gas through an SUV, that had sent her straight to the bubbly. She'd always lacked intestinal fortitude.

"That must have been nice." Kathryn's face said she knew otherwise.

"I'm certain you did well," Ethan contributed to humor her along.

Zoe grimaced. What a disappointment she'd be to her beloved Mummy and Pop and pompous old Rags if they could see her now, employed as a second-rate gossip columnist and often flat broke because she'd pledged to make do on her meager salary to protect the remaining trust fund.

"I'm not quite the raging success they expected," she admitted. The couple had been kind but noticeably taken aback by her chosen profession.

"Stuffy snobs," Ethan said. "Never mind." He dropped a hand on Zoe's bare shoulder the way her pop used to, both encouraging and proud, while she'd bent over her textbooks as a dorky, bespectacled fifteen-year-old studying for her college entrance exams.

That version of Zoe Aberdeen was as long gone as her family.

Ethan, the incorrigible flirt, gave her a teasing brush of his fingers before moving off. "I ought to be on my way before we draw attention from the tower."

The managing editor presided over the lesser columnists and reporters from a spacious second-floor corner glass office with a mezzanine that overlooked the newsroom. Editors like Kathryn had been granted similar but smaller offices on the exterior rim of the ground floor. Zoe's space was at the approximate center of the room, a magnet for anyone in need of chocolate, a dirty joke or a bit of juicy gossip.

Kathryn gripped the steel edge of the cubicle wall. "What's that you've got?"

Zoe looked down. Clasped to her chest was one of the many lucky charms that cluttered the desk, a folk art figurine. She must have picked it up for reassurance. "It's that voodoo doll I bought in the Gaslamp Quarter weeks ago."

"I remember. The day we discovered the lust potion." Kathryn came around the partition, steering an unoccupied desk chair so she could sit knee to knee inside Zoe's cubicle. "It's an ugly old thing, isn't it?"

"I kind of like her." The pocket-size voodoo doll wasn't as crude as some. Mayan symbols had been carved into the figure's bulbous body.

Kathryn turned the doll over with long, deft fingers. "Solid ebony. Where do you stick the pins?"

Zoe raised her brows. "Thinking of cursing someone?"

The book editor shrugged. Her relationship with Coyote Sullivan had veered wildly between adversarial and erotic for the past month or so. But ever since her return from a recent vacation that was *supposed* to be solo, she'd been glowing, and not only because of the newly acquired tan.

Nope, Zoe knew a mama-got-sex glow when she saw one, even on such an uncharacteristic place as Kath's face. Which made her wonder just how effective one small filched sample of lust potion could possibly be.

"I don't believe this is a voodoo doll at all," Kathryn said, handing it over. "With such massive breasts, perhaps it's meant to be a fertility symbol?"

Zoe threw up her hands, refusing the doll. "Perish the thought." She had a reputation to maintain, one where marriage and babies were the very last things she should desire.

"I don't want it either." Kathryn set the doll on the desk. "Especially after the lust potion turned out to be…" She shook her head, saying no more.

Zoe thought the purported lust potion was a fascinating topic. "Especially after the potion made you and Coyote do the horizontal rumba until you were both howling at the moon?"

"It didn't *make* us. Or at least we don't know for certain that it did." Kathryn didn't bother to hide a satisfied smile. "Nor were we always horizontal."

Zoe chuckled. "So you're saying that you made a conscious decision to engage in an affair so hot it's capable of burning down the *Times* building?"

Kathryn's eyes twinkled. "Please restrict the hyperbole to your column."

"This isn't for my column." Zoe wrote about local celebrities, society debs and the forays of Hollywood bigwigs who'd drifted south to engage in San Diego's laid-back lifestyle. In other words, fluff and flattery. "I'm thinking of doing an investigative piece."

"On the potion?"

Zoe's headache was subsiding, so she risked a nod. *"Balam K'am-bi,"* she intoned. "The lust potion of the gods."

Kathryn chimed in. "From deep in the heart of the Yucatan…"

"Comes this elixir…"

"That brings the world's greatest sexual experience…" Kathryn pinkened at the word *sexual*.

"To the person who dares to use it," Zoe finished. Although they treated their belief in the lust potion as a joke, a folly, Kath had confessed that the effect on her had been too real to discount.

Zoe intended to find out why.

A while back, she, Kathryn and Ethan had been wandering the Gaslamp district during their lunch break, noshing and joshing, when they'd found a funky tourist trap called Jag's on one of the side streets. They had heard rumors about a sleazy little man selling a knockoff lust potion to the tourists while dealing the genuine, very pricey concoction to a select upper-crust clientele. The shopkeeper had given them a spiel about the origins of *Balam K'am-bi,* promising hot sex, multiple orgasms, yada yada, which none of them had believed. Then.

A police cruiser had been pulling up to the shop as the trio was leaving. Later Zoe had discovered that a vial of *Balam K'am-bi* had been planted in her bag. Surmising that Jag had done so to remove the evidence from his possession, Ethan had volunteered to bring the lust potion to the cops for analysis. The official police response had been underwhelming.

The incident might have ended there if Kathryn hadn't later admitted to retaining a small sample of the potion for her own experimentation. An explosive, completely out-of-character experimentation, judging by the bits and pieces Zoe had gleaned about Kathryn's hot-cha-cha relationship with Coyote Sullivan.

Even so, Zoe remained doubtful. She'd sensed an attraction between Kathryn and Coyote long before the venture to Jag's. Their affair was not unexpected.

Kath's loss of inhibition could also be explained. The power of suggestion and all that.

But *something* was going on. Jag wouldn't have slipped the potion into Zoe's bag if the vial had contained a harmless liquid. Considering the heightening of physical sensation some users had reported, she suspected the potion contained an illegal extract. Perhaps one that produced a tingling warmth similar to those provided by certain intimate sexual lotions currently on the market.

"I wish I'd thought to keep my own sample of the lust potion," Zoe mused. "You wouldn't happen to have any left over?"

Kathryn shrugged. "Sorry."

Zoe eyed her. "You used every drop?"

"I had a very small amount."

"And it's all gone?"

Kathryn mumbled under her breath, not letting Zoe pin her down.

Too modest to give details, Zoe wondered, or the opposite? She took a not-so-wild guess. "So that's why you're never around lately. Still keeping extra busy with Coyote, hmm?"

"Oh, well, you know how we were competing for the Crest of the Wave award," Kathryn said, intentionally misunderstanding.

Excuses. She'd won the prestigious editors' prize weeks ago, although the announcement had been eclipsed by the furor caused when Coyote broke the story of a pro football steroids scandal. Threats and pressure from all sides had resulted in his tendering his resignation to the newspaper.

Zoe pressed. "You *are* still together?"

"Not for publication." Kath grinned. "But, yes."

Before Zoe could ask more, her friend stood and made a quick adjustment of her skirt. Kathryn was clad in the usual dark business suit, though Zoe had caught a glimpse of a lacy bra when the loose neckline of Kathryn's shell had gaped. Bronze-colored tendrils had escaped from the book editor's hair clip. Her lips and cheeks were bright pink against the glowy tan.

All very suspicious.

I've got to find out what was in that bottle. Zoe was rarely so determined, but the humiliation of running into the Aberdeens' family friends had convinced her to improve her situation in life. While the job at the *Times* had been a much-needed stopgap, it wasn't too late to become a person of whom her family would have been proud.

Put in that light, staking her chances on a bogus lust potion didn't seem to be the smartest move.

"'Lust potion of the gods,'" she quoted. "Gimme a break."

Kathryn delayed her departure. "Have you tried a Web search?"

"Of course. I found a few unsubstantiated reports of the potion's effects and some references to the Mayan dialect. As we already knew, *Balam K'am-bi* roughly translates to *sex of the jaguar.*"

"Wild animal sex," Kathryn said faintly, her eyes distant.

"Hot jungle lovin'," Zoe teased.

Kathryn blinked. "You should ask Ethan. He's the one with all the police connections."

The women exchanged knowing smiles. Ethan's connection to one police detective in particular—an attractive female named Nicole Arroyo—had become obvious despite his attempts at discretion. They'd even begun to speculate that the confirmed bachelor might have finally met his match.

"I tried," Zoe said. "He claimed that Detective Arroyo had sent our sample to the crime lab but there were no results yet. I don't suppose the case is considered urgent enough to warrant a rush job."

"Keep me informed. I'd like to hear what that report says." Kathryn returned the extra chair to the neighboring cubicle. "See you at lunch." She strode away, clearly making an effort to appear as businesslike as ever but not quite able to restrain the sassy swing of her hips.

Zoe fingered the native doll. There was no doubt about it. Kathryn Walters was a changed woman.

Due to the lust potion?

Although titillated by the idea, Zoe's primary interest

wasn't the personal benefits of the supposed aphrodi-
siac. This time, she preferred to be taken seriously.

If she could get the real story on the lust potion, she
might gain a little respect at the newspaper, proving to
Barbie the Editrix she could write about more than
champagne fountains and oysters on the half shell. Or
she might submit a feature article to a national magazine. She could do background research in Mexico,
interview scientists, track down unlikely couples such
as Kathryn and Coyote, maybe even turn the story into
a book. Even gain interest from Hollywood.

Granted, none of that was likely to win her a Pulitzer,
but at least she'd have some proof that she hadn't completely wasted her potential.

But where to begin?

"Go to the source," Zoe told herself.

Fortunately the ibuprofen had kicked in. She leaned
down and picked up the leather Hermès carryall she'd
dropped under her desk and started shoveling necessary
items inside. The BlackBerry, her trusty notebook, a
spare pair of sneakers in case she had to walk farther
than heels allowed. She checked the contents of her
wallet. A coupon for a facial, plus two dollars and
change. Damn. Last time she'd gone to the cash
machine, the printout of her balance had been so
alarming she'd survived on tuna, crackers and olives
ever since.

Plus hors d'oeuvres and champagne. No wonder she
was feeling dizzy.

Ignoring her queasy stomach, Zoe counted out

enough coins to buy a bag of potato chips from the vending machine. Her paycheck wasn't due for a few days. After work, she'd hit Zanzibar's happy-hour buffet for free Buffalo wings and jalapeño poppers.

In the meantime, making headway on her goal would give her mood a better boost than protein.

As funding a trip to the Yucatan wasn't in the credit cards, she had only two immediate options. One was to acquire a copy of the crime-lab analysis of the lust potion. Luckily she had a great contact in that system—a nerdy neighbor across the hall in her apartment building. They didn't exactly get along, but if necessary, she'd use her feminine wiles to beguile him into helping her out. The other immediate option was to return to Jag's tourist trap and get the story from the lizard's mouth, so to speak.

Zoe being Zoe, she chose to do both ASAP.

2

DONOVAN SHANE TENDED TO become overly absorbed by his work. He'd managed to ignore the annoying buzz of the intercom system, but he was forced out of his fog when Guillermo Reyes opened the door to the toxicology lab and cleared his throat.

"Dr. Shane, Mandy Rae says to tell you there's a *woman* here to see you," the intern announced in a tone of awe, as if he'd never seen such a creature. The kid was a senior in high school; he should have had girls crawling out of his locker.

Donovan squinted as he pinched the skin at the bridge of his nose. He'd been examining the peaks on the liquid chromatograph done on a sample from a murder case. "Whoever she is, she doesn't have an appointment."

"She's…" At a loss for words, Guillermo gave an exceptionally gusty exhale. His sinuses tended to whistle when he got overexcited. "Damn, boss, you gotta see her."

Boss. Donovan had never been a boss before. After earning his undergraduate degree, he'd been rejected by the police academy because of a preexisting condition—the heart murmur he'd had since childhood—and had taken a part-time lab technician's job instead while advancing toward his Ph.D. Twelve years later, he was still working in the same facility, now as a toxicologist specializing in the typing and analysis of blood and other fluids. He told himself that he was satisfied to be left alone in the lab, quietly doing his job analyzing the minutiae of crime while others ran about like over-adrenalized superheroes, shooting at perps and risking their lives.

"Is she a kook?" he asked.

"I dunno. Maybe." The intern gripped the doorknob. "She claims she knows you. Says she won't leave until you see her."

Shoulders hunched, Donovan returned to his study of the graph on the computer screen. He wasn't keen to leave his work and make the trip to the reception desk in the lobby, where all visitors must check in before gaining admittance. He couldn't imagine who this one-of-a-kind female might be.

Sadly he didn't know many women. There was Mandy Rae, the pretty receptionist who tolerated him and the rest of the lab rats with unconcealed distaste. Lucilla, the facility's cleaning lady, who griped at him for filling his wastebaskets and using all the paper towels. A small handful of female police officers, whom he spoke to mainly on the phone when they were anxious for urgent results of the evidence they'd couriered over. He supposed he had to include Dr. Victoria Eubanks, the comely optometrist he'd dated for five months until she'd told him, in the middle of his second eye exam that year, that she'd decided to go back to the ex-husband who'd cheated on her with his secretary.

Lastly, but never leastly, there was Zoe Aberdeen.

His neighbor.

His sworn nemesis.

His greatest fantasy.

Zoe? Could it be? Donovan's head shot up so fast he lost his balance in the ensuing blood rush. *Zoe. Of course.* A wayward elbow knocked into a hydrometer jar that had been shifted from its appointed position. Zoe Aberdeen was *exactly* the type of woman who could make a goofus like Guillermo misplace his brain.

Donovan moved the jar back into place. Not to mention a goofus like himself.

"You didn't answer Mandy Rae's summons," Guillermo explained, "so she sent me to tell you." The intern was almost blithering as he peered out at the hallway, apparently expecting an invasion. "She said for you to come see because she's not allowed to send unscheduled visitors to the lab with all the new protocols and—oh, jeezus, boss, here she is."

Donovan shoved up his cuffs as he made for the door. He was betting the "she" wasn't Mandy Rae, who turned up her nose at the pungent and occasionally gruesome smells wafting from the lab.

Sure enough, Zoe Aberdeen in all her glory sashayed up the staircase and through the hallway, as tricked out as a Mardi Gras celebrant. Most women would be overwhelmed by that particular combination of curly red hair, orange tank top and flared denim miniskirt, all of it topped off by bangles, chains and jewels swinging off every appendage.

But Zoe Aberdeen wasn't most women.

Mandy Rae raced to catch up, waving a visitors' badge. "Dr. Shane! I'm sorry. I got her to sign in, but she slipped past the door while I was making up the badge."

"It's all right," he said. "I know her."

"What a lot of fuss." Zoe planted her heels and put her hands on her hips. "What's going on back here, Shane? State secrets?"

"In a manner of speaking." Donovan resettled his wire-frame glasses. You always had to squint and blink when Zoe arrived. "I'm afraid you can't stay. The labs are off-limits to most civilians."

Zoe took the laminated badge from Mandy Rae and clamped it to her spaghetti strap. "Civilians?" A gay laugh. "Do I appear civilized to you, Shane? How disappointing." An incorrigible flirt, she looked at Guillermo with a moue of her full, glossy lips. There had to be a beauty product that made them look that way. No normal lips were quite so wet and plump and kissable. "I promise you, sweetcakes, I'm as wild as they come."

She pointed a long red fingernail at Donovan. "And *he* should know. Remind me, Shane. How many times have you called the cops on me?"

He cleared his throat. "Twice."

"Only twice? I thought it was at least a half dozen." She lowered her sunglasses to the end of her nose and slinked toward him with the hippy, shoulder-rolling saunter that was often featured—nude—in his dreams. Mandy Rae watched, fascinated. "Have you been lying to me, Shane, honey, all those times you said I'd better shut down the party because you'd called the cops?"

He held his spot. "I said I *would* call the cops."

"And twice you did."

"My walls were shaking."

She sent him an unapologetic grin as she brushed by him on her way into the lab. Waving off Mandy Rae, Donovan followed on Zoe's heels, intending to stay nearby so she didn't touch any of the sensitive evidence that he kept scrupulously labeled and filed.

He stood so close he could smell her. She was sweet, but not from perfume. Zoe's scent carried the sweetness of sugar—jelly beans, cherry licorice sticks, birthday cakes, fluffy pink cotton candy. All the forbidden treats he hadn't been allowed as a sickly child.

Looking around the room and his adjoining office with airy interest, she removed her sunglasses and hooked them in the neckline of the skimpy top. He kept pace, practically peering over her shoulder, his hands itching to grab hold and keep her still. He didn't quite dare. Zoe was too light and fluttery. He was too clumsy. A butterfly net would do a better job of containing her.

Suddenly she stopped and whirled to face him. "So this is the big secret?" Her head tilted. Her eyes were bright. "Looks like every other lab I've seen. In another life, I was a geek, too."

"You were not." Not in a million years.

She abandoned the claim with a lift of her bare

shoulders, regarding his dumbstruck face with a small, teasing smile. She moved an inch closer and stroked a finger downward from the knot of his tie. He'd tucked the ends in between his shirt buttons, so there wasn't far to go.

Her polished nail lifted the edge of his shirt placket. She peered inside at the protected tie. Her narrow nose wrinkled. "You're so prissy, Shane. Like an old maid."

She always called him Shane. He liked that, though he couldn't pinpoint why.

Old maid was less flattering. He felt himself becoming huffy and defensive, the way he often did around Zoe. She was far too unpredictable for his personal comfort zone. And he worried he'd give away some clue about how often he fantasized about her. "Precision is crucial to a scientist."

Her frank stare ran over him. "I thought you'd be in a lab coat. I always picture you in a lab coat. Which is kind of funny since I've never seen you in one." Her smile was wide and inexplicably charming. She knew it, too. Knew it and used it, in concert with a wide-eyed blink that was quite versatile. Innocent-sexy or devilish-sexy or sassy-sexy. But always sexy.

He'd never noticed that her eyes were the color of maple syrup, flecked with gold leaf. Always before, she'd been coming or going, shouting down the stairwell or waving at him from their shared backyard, where she liked to sunbathe topless. She wasn't shy about turning over onto her back, either. He might not have known the color of her eyes, but he was well acquainted with her breasts. They were the proverbial martini-glass tits —small and pert. Lightly freckled. Her nipples were bubblegum-pink when they hardened.

"I have a lab coat," he blurted. "Over there."

"So I see." Her steep platform clogs clacked on the floor as she crossed the room to the row of pegs where black rubber aprons, safety goggles and lab coats hung. "Can I try it on? Or is that like trying on a cowboy's hat?"

"What?"

"You know. Wear my hat, try me on." She winked and slipped into the shapeless white coat.

Except it wasn't shapeless on her, even though her slender figure was swallowed by the starched white cotton folds. The coat completely covered her own clothing. There was something erotic about seeing her bare legs beneath the crisp hem, especially when he glimpsed a thigh in the unbuttoned gap. As if she might be naked underneath.

Add the notion she'd put in his head that he could have allowance to slip as easily into *her* and—

Brain freeze.

But fever everywhere else. He tugged at his collar, then an ear. Other areas needed more intimate adjustment. He was thirty-three years old, for crying out loud. He hadn't had such a swift and awkward boner since high school. No, make that since his one and only spring-break trip to Mexico, when he'd learned that alcohol magically untied the bikini straps of cute college coeds.

Zoe twirled, kicking up a heel. "What do you think?"

"Nice," Donovan croaked. That was all he could

think of to say, because her twirl had lifted the edge of the coat and the ruffle on her flirty little skirt, flashing him a glimpse of a taut bottom clad in a pair of zebra-stripe bikini panties. *Boing.*

Guillermo's jaw hung slack.

"This has been fun, but I came to ask for a favor," Zoe said when neither of the men spoke. Her voice had taken on an unusual gravitas.

Donovan was both intrigued and disappointed. How many times had cute females like Zoe flirted with him, only to ask for something two seconds later, from copying his chemistry homework to requesting over-night lab results?

She shrugged out of the coat as she walked toward the lab bench, the solid table they worked on. Her sharp eyes made a quick survey of the contents. "I'm writing a story for the *Times.*"

"But you're a gossip columnist." Donovan read her twice-a-week columns even though most of the names and faces meant nothing to him, not unlike the details of what they wore and where they partied. "Excuse me. I should introduce you to my intern. Zoe Aberdeen, Guillermo Reyes. She works for the *San Diego Times.*"

The boy nodded with glazed eyes. He was six inches taller than Zoe and almost twice her weight, but he was thrown for such a loop by her presence that she could have hog-tied him without a squeak of protest. Donovan knew the feeling.

Zoe twiddled her fingers at Guillermo. *"Ciao."* To

Donovan, she said with a highly arched brow, "I may be a gossipmonger, but I'm also a journalist."

"Oh. Yes, of course. Did you study journalism?"

"I have a master's in literature. Before everything changed, I was planning to find a nice, cozy position as a teaching assistant so I could expand on my thesis, but, uh—" She broke off and, oddly tongue-tied, looked down at the material her hands were wadding.

Donovan waited, so curious about her claims that he didn't even consider taking the coat from her to shake out the wrinkles.

"But that's not relevant," she continued with a frown. "My degree isn't in journalism anyway." Her eyes rose to Donovan, narrowing as she threw out one of her typically unexpected remarks. "Do you only answer the questions of those with the proper pedigree?"

"Of course not." He was still trying to absorb the news that Zoe had an advanced degree of any sort. From what he knew of her, with the string of boyfriends and the loud parties and the comings and goings at all hours, she was strictly the Holly Go-lightly of the West Coast, dedicated to burning her candle at both ends.

"That's good, because I need—"

He interrupted her request. "Sorry. I turn *everyone* away, regardless of their credentials. This lab's test results aren't for public consumption."

"What about if it's a case of the public good? Like something dangerously contagious?"

"In that case, I suspect the *Times* wouldn't send a gossip columnist to investigate."

Her pointy chin jutted at him. "But what if they did?"

"Doesn't matter. I don't make those decisions. You can get in touch with the police department's press liaison and ask your questions there."

Zoe flung his coat at the table. It hit the edge and slid to the floor. Spots of color had flared in her cheeks. "Why do you work so hard at making me dislike you, Donovan Shane? I've tried to be friendly, but you're distant and implacable. Dry as dust. You have no—" Her hands flew up in the air. "No *zest!*"

"I'm not an orange."

She blew out a sigh. "You're also too literal."

"I was making a joke. A bad one, granted."

Her gaze zeroed in on him and she was silent for several seconds—an eternity for Zoe. He feared what might come next, but she asked mildly, "Do you always frown when you're trying to be humorous?"

His answering frown was automatic. "I don't know."

"Interesting. I've never known you to crack a joke." Her lips puckered. "It appears that you have unplumbed depths, Shane."

"Likewise, Aberdeen."

She took another moment to evaluate him. The gradual, sensual lowering of her coppery lashes was only slightly less distracting than the pouty lips. His blood thickened.

"Sooo, Shane, what can I do to get you to give me a peek at a substance-analysis report?"

"Nothing." He shook his head. Or at least he thought he did. There was very little feeling left in his body outside of the blast furnace that had developed in his groin. For propriety's sake, he shifted until he'd put the lab bench between them.

"There's got to be something. Tickets for the Chargers. Uncensored candids of the Ocean Beach women's volleyball tournament. A backstage pass to Shakira in concert."

A soft, bubbling groan came from Guillermo's direction. Although twenty pounds overweight and prone to sloppiness, he was a well-meaning kid who worked a couple of hours several mornings a week, washing beakers, labeling files and losing track of hydrometer jars. He planned to major in chemistry when he went to San Diego State next fall.

Donovan remained stalwart. "I won't be bribed."

Zoe glanced at the intern.

"Don't even think about it, Gil."

She laughed. "I was only wondering if I could speak to you in, um…" She put her hands flat on the bench top and leaned toward Donovan. A few of the cascading curls fell into her eyes. Her voice lowered. "In private."

His gaze flicked to the spot where the weight of her sunglasses dragged at the orange tank top. Her freckled cleavage was modest compared to the silicone valleys that populated the city. But powerful nevertheless. "Gil…"

"I'm out of here."

Donovan had meant to ask the intern to stay, but he let the words die on his tongue.

While Guillermo hastily departed, Zoe leaned farther over the table to push at a file folder with one finger, flicking it open.

Donovan suspected he was supposed to be mesmer-

ized by her feminine wiles, but he wasn't quite that far
a goner. He whisked the stack of files away, then rescued
his clipboard, no longer certain that she couldn't understand the forms it held. That possibility was almost as
tantalizing as her cleavage.

She lifted her chin to stare broodingly at him. "Tell
me the truth now. Did you send Gil away so we could
be alone?"

Surely she was joking. "What?" he said, feeling
awkward and shy. High school all over again.

Her smile became mischievous. "You're cute when
you're worried. I'm only curious about how the lab
operates. Do others work here?"

She'd managed to put him off center again. He collected his thoughts. "This is the toxicology lab. Today
I was alone except when Gil came by for an hour. I do
have a colleague who's out on maternity leave. And
there are plenty of other employees in the building,
working in other labs or offices, technicians with different specialties. We share some of the equipment." He
paused. "They can pop in at any time."

"My goodness. That was a thorough answer. You'd
think I was suggesting something naughtier than giving
me a peek at an analysis."

He wouldn't let himself think about what he wanted
a peek at. "I'm not relenting," he said, "but what's this
about, this result you're so eager to read?"

She straightened, giving him a provocative look. "It's
about sexual enhancement." Her voice had taken on the
rough velvet of a cat's purr.

He gaped. "What?"

"I want to know if the lust potion works." Her brows arched wickedly. "And *you* are the only man who can help me."

3

"WHAT'S WRONG, SHANE? Cat got your tongue?"

He continued staring.

Zoe waved a hand in front of his face, feeling fine and sassy. She could wrap Donovan Shane, nerd scientist, around her pinkie with very little effort. Amazing how the adrenaline of female power had cured the lingering effects of her hangover.

He brushed her away. "How do you know about the lust—" Suddenly he had to clear his throat. "How do you know about the *alleged* lust potion?"

"It's not a secret. Jag's been selling it to the tourists for months."

"Jag?"

"I presume. We don't know his real name. He runs this seedy little shop in the Gaslamp that sells the lust potion. Along with voodoo dolls, cheap beads, amulets and charms, carved tchotchkes—whatever." She shrugged. "I've been there. I was the one who—"

"Not that." Shane dismissed her in that autocratic way of his. The man really did make her hackles rise. He was so rigid, even when she'd "discombobulated" him. "I meant how did you know I was testing a lust potion?"

"If you'd let me finish…" She fished out another deliberate smile, remembering that she needed a favor from him no matter how irritating he was. "I was the one who turned the potion over to the police."

"You?" Shane's eyes flickered behind his wire-framed glasses. "Then you've already tried the potion?"

She'd love to tell him that, yes, the loud activity he'd recently heard coming from her apartment had been the result of headboard-banging hot monkey love and not the installation of a shelf in her closet after an overloaded one had collapsed. But that would be dishonest.

She didn't have any problem with telling white lies. It was only that she preferred to do so to gain an advantage.

And Shane *already* believed she was a sex-crazed party girl.

Zoe drew herself up. So what if the assumption wasn't completely wrong? She'd rather have too much fun than none at all.

She aimed another sultry gaze his way. "If I'd tried it, Shane, I would know if it worked."

He cranked his head back, as if looking at her required a distance between them. He'd probably slide her under a microscope if he could. "Maybe it worked and you couldn't tell a difference?"

Was that another joke?

She tossed her curls. "Maybe. I do like to have a good time."

"You don't have to tell me. We share a bedroom wall." Zoe thought he was about to smile, but he shook his head instead, scoffing at her. "Don't tell me you actually believe in this hokum about a lust potion?"

"I didn't. Until I heard the stories."

"Stories? Gossip, I suppose."

Annoying man. She crossed her arms, glaring at him even though she should be flirting. Whenever they got near each other, he bristled at her teasing and she ended up wishing she could take the starch out of him by any means necessary. "You have a problem with my job?"

"Why should I?" He peered at her, making her squirm. "It suits you."

Counting to ten, she stopped at four. "I doubt you mean that as a compliment."

"What do you think?"

"That if you consider me mere window dressing, you shouldn't have a problem sharing what you know about the potion."

He took off his glasses and polished them with the end of the tie he'd liberated from his shirtfront. His forehead had creased. Without the glasses, he seemed more vulnerable and rather boyishly awkward in his confusion over how to deal with her. She realized that his huffiness was a defense mechanism. And that he had thick lashes, a well-shaped mouth and might be rather sexy if he'd stop acting like a prude.

"I'm sorry if I gave you the wrong impression." He glanced at her with softened eyes, his brows turning up in the middle. "I'm sure you give pleasure to many people. Your columns, I mean." His gaze dropped to her body, then bounced back up as he turned a dull shade of red. "It's just that you have this way of, um—" He put on the glasses and ran his fingers through a short crop of brown hair as he looked away. "You get under my skin."

"Because I'm so loud and outlandish?"

"You are, but no."

This time when he looked at her, she saw the naked desire he'd suppressed. A sexual hunger seethed in him so viscerally that she felt it melting into her, too.

But he wasn't her type! He was quiet and conventional and brainy and dull—

A hot spike of inexplicable emotion went straight through her. "Don't look at me that way," she blurted, confused by her reaction. The idea of having sex with Shane should have been laughable instead of disconcerting. "I'm not who you think I am."

"That sounds like a warning." He scowled. "So when you said I was the only man who could help you with the lust potion…?"

"Oh!" She blinked a couple of times, trying to resist studying his face as if she'd never seen him before. There'd always been a sort of unpolished manliness about him. A well-hidden potential. Even so, she'd never considered him in *that* way, at least not seriously.

This time she couldn't help herself. She looked. And the heat in his dark eyes flowed through her. She could feel her cheeks coloring to match his. "You thought I wanted…"

He thought I was offering to participate in a very intimate lab experiment.

Zoe couldn't decide whether to be amused or aroused.

Objectively, with his lean, rangy body and a face that was all nose and high cheekbones, Donovan Shane was not unappealing. Under the right circumstances, he could melt her like butter. But he was always so stiff around her, verging on antagonistic. Even if that was only a defense, a front to hide his insecurities—and, boy, she knew all about *those*—there was still no reason for her to be flustered by his hoping she'd give him a jump.

Of course, she'd suspected all along that secretly he thought she was sexy. The signals were obvious no matter how hard he tried to conceal them. She'd simply assumed that he'd go on fighting the attraction to a woman who was obviously not his type.

Apparently he was willing to lose the battle.

To test a lust potion he didn't believe in?

Which meant his motivation was *her.*

Zoe was uncomfortable. While she was willing to charm her way in and out of sticky situations, she didn't want to be responsible for Shane's interests *that* way.

And yet…

And yet the way he was watching her made her nerves jangle. She felt like a top that had been spinning tightly in its place and was now wobbling out of control as it slowed.

She set her fists on top of the table. Giving over control wasn't her strong suit. What she couldn't manage, she avoided, starting with the day she'd run away from her duties as the last of the Aberdeens.

"I'm looking into the validity of the lust potion," she said, her voice thick in her throat as she restated her objective to skim by the past few moments of sheer lunacy that might be a mutual attraction, even a *potent* one. "And I would very much appreciate it if you'd do me this one tiny, little favor and share the results of your tests."

Shane opened his mouth, but she overrode him. "I know you have the sample. My friend Ethan Ramsey, the newspaper's crime reporter, was the one who turned the potion over to Detective Arroyo when we first became suspicious."

"I can't—"

"But it was *mine*." She skipped past the detail that Jag had planted the vial in her purse. "I did the responsible thing by seeing that the potion went to the authorities. Don't I deserve special consideration?" She brought the tips of two fingers together. "Just a little?"

Shane remained unmoved. "You should have retained a sample. Then you could have taken it to a commercial lab for your own analysis."

"We didn't think of that." She shrugged. "At the time, my friends and I didn't seriously believe that the potion might be real."

"You said you had suspicions."

"That was only because of the officers that swarmed the shop as we were leaving. I guess there had been complaints about the product being a rip-off, so they were checking out the story." She ground her teeth. She had to persuade him to help her out. "There have been actual symptoms since then, symptoms we can't explain."

"Symptoms of lust." Shane crossed his arms. "Uh-huh. I'll bet *those* are hard to come by in your world."

"I've seen it with my own eyes." If she counted Kathryn and Coyote as evidence.

Shane's jaw, already firm, clenched even more. "But you haven't experienced the effect yourself?"

"No."

He waved a dismissal. "Then it's all hearsay. That doesn't cut it for me. Or a court of law."

"No one's being prosecuted." *Yet,* she added silently, thinking of the cruiser arriving at Jag's shop. She made a mental note to interview Detective Arroyo about the progress of the investigation.

"Doesn't matter," Shane said. "The lust potion is still in police custody. There may be charges pending."

"The case can't be very important if you haven't analyzed the potion yet."

"Who says I haven't?"

She narrowed her eyes. "Me." She glanced around the organized yet crowded room. The tables, desks and shelves were jammed with scientific accoutrements, including computers, microscopes, scales, a centrifuge and several impressive machines that were far more advanced than her knowledge. A large industrial waste can was labeled with a biohazard sign. She was most interested in the racks of beakers and test tubes that sat near a humming industrial steel freezer. "Where is the potion? On ice? Can I see it at least?"

His eyes went straight to one of the racks. He'd be a lousy poker player. "You've already seen it, so how would that help?"

She strolled past the central lab table. "Never mind. I can look for it myself. I'm sure it's labeled."

Shane moved with a swift athleticism she hadn't expected out of him but should have, considering how often he went bicycling. If she'd looked past the dorky helmet and knee pads, she'd have noticed the muscles in his long legs and tight butt.

"Keep away," he said. "Don't touch. I have a chain of evidence to protect."

He put his hands on her shoulders. She instantly froze. The warmth and strength of his grip was also surprising. A soft, gloppy weakness dropped through her, buckling her knees before she caught herself and snapped back to her center of balance.

"I won't touch," she promised, sounding less certain than she intended because she'd gone slightly breathless. She gestured at a vial at random. "Is that it? Have you smelled it?"

"I've already freeze-dried the samples. I used the chemical fume hood, although I was told the substance has no scent." Reaching past her, he picked up a labeled beaker and pried off the top. "This is the excess of the second sample, the one that you claim was yours before your reporter friend turned it in."

Zoe barely withheld her shiver. For a brief moment, Shane's chest had pressed against the back of her shoulders. Not a particularly erogenous zone of hers—until now. She was accustomed to men brushing against her, trying to get familiar, even copping a feel. This was the first time an inadvertent touch had cut through her nervous system like the screech of feedback from a microphone.

"I shouldn't do this, but…" He took a whiff. "Nothing. No smell."

"May I?"

He held the beaker before her face. The liquid inside appeared clear at first glance, but there was a very faint pink shimmer, almost a sparkle, when she tilted her nose toward it. She sniffed.

And smelled nothing, as Shane had said.

"Wait." She placed her hand over his when he attempted to withdraw the beaker. She tried again, inhaling long and deep. Even with no actual scent, the potion was indefinably alluring.

Her eyes closed. There seemed to be a significance, but the substance of it remained frustratingly out of reach, like a distant mist in the jungle.

Her nostrils tingled. Her lips became soft, full, as if awaiting a kiss. The longing for contact throbbed at her pulse points, and she tightened her hold on Shane's hand, drawing him into herself.

"Zoe." His voice was deliciously rough in her ear as he pressed against her to set down the beaker. "Tell me about these symptoms of lust."

Her eyes widened. He didn't feel it!

How could he *not* feel it?

His fingers moved against her bare shoulder. Almost stroking. The gust of his healthy exhale stirred her hair.

Perhaps he did feel it.

She licked her lips. "My friend Kathryn tried the potion. She said it gave her an actual physical reaction."

Shane's fingertips grazed her shoulder blades, creating a trail of sizzling sensation that danced across her skin before his hands fell away. "Which was?"

"Warmth, escalating to intense heat. Tingling. She said her brain got kind of foggy. She lost her reason."

"Not unusual feelings." He adjusted his glasses. "In an intimate situation."

Her lips curled into a teasing grin as she turned to face him. "Especially when you're with the right person."

Or with an entirely unexpected person.

Neither moved. Heat radiated between them. A blush colored the jut of Shane's cheekbones. Very faintly, but an honest-to-goodness blush, which didn't go with his severe man-of-science persona but did fit the geeky boy-ishness she'd glimpsed when he'd taken off his glasses.

"I think Kath even tasted the potion," Zoe heard herself saying. "She didn't give me the more carnal details, but apparently the effect was astounding. And immediate." She considered. "Maybe I'll volunteer to be your guinea pig. Just a tiny taste, do you think? I'm sure nothing too alarming will happen. You can observe me. In a detached, scientific way, of course."

Speaking all those words had limbered her numb tongue. She curled it against the back of her teeth, barely able to resist the desire to flick it across Shane's firm lips. Would he be surprised if she kissed him?

Once, perhaps. No more. You'd have to be made of stone not to feel what was going on here. Granted, she had accused him of just that. But she'd been wrong. Shane was human. Very human. As prone to temptation as a fat man with a cupcake, judging by the devouring hunger of his stare.

Her body temperature kicked up another degree. The air was so tense she expected it to crackle when she stroked a palm over his pinstriped shirtfront. Alas, he fell short of true nerd-dom. There weren't even any pockets for protectors.

She poked at his chest. "No protection."

"Pardon?" The look on his face said that he was thinking *condom* while she was thinking *Revenge of the Nerds.*

She bit her lip, stopping the silly giggle that tickled her throat.

What was wrong with her? She reveled in silly giggles. Could it be that, despite the lust potion, she wanted him to be impressed by her smarts instead of dazzled by her body?

"Zoe." Shane's face showed the struggle to stay detached. "Experimenting without, um, safeguards is not a good idea."

"What's the fun in that? Don't you ever try something that you know is a bad idea, just for the adventure of it?" She pressed a knuckle on the knot of his tie and flicked at his chin with one finger. "Do you *always* behave?"

He jerked his head out of reach, but he didn't retreat. "Yes, I do. That's the way I was raised."

"Oh, how sad." She didn't admit she'd grown up the same way, with schoolbooks for companions and flash cards for fun. Why spoil the illusion when she was unsure about where she wanted this to go? "I should teach you how to misbehave."

"Starting with the lust potion I suppose." He inhaled, his chest rising beneath her arm. "You're trying to distract me again, aren't you?"

"Is it working?"

"More than it should. I know better."

The intense feeling of *needing* to touch him had ebbed slightly. "Let's start here," she said, loosening the tie with a few quick movements. She stepped away, dragging out the knot until the tie dangled freely against his chest. "There. Now you can breathe without choking."

He stroked the tie, because she had. A poor substitute for touching her, but Donovan couldn't allow himself any more leeway. With her beguiling ways and sexy little body, Zoe was the drug—not the lust potion.

He'd come within a hair's breadth of handing over the remaining sample. Not because he believed the potion was legitimate. The odds were that she could have poured it over his head without consequence.

Some other time, she could have.

Right now, his lust was already off the charts.

Hers, however, could use some encouraging in his direction. While her flirtation had been well played, he hadn't been fooled into believing that she truly wanted him.

But if he gave her the potion…

Where the hell had that idea come from? He *never* broke the rules of the lab.

He lurched away from her, rubbing a hand across his forehead. *Think, man. Anything to get her out of here before you turn into a complete buffoon.*

"I suppose I can give you a—a tip. After the results come in." That was safe, since there'd be nothing to report except that there was nothing to report.

"Thanks." She beamed. "When they print my article and I'm famous, I'll call you an anonymous source."

"If that makes you happy." He shrugged. "Be warned— I'm not putting a rush job on this for your benefit."

"We'll see." Zoe winked as if she believed he'd be chugging the potion like Dr. Jekyll the instant she departed. With a waggle of her red fingernails, she flounced out of the lab. "*Ciao,* handsome. I'll be in touch."

Donovan leaned his fists against the lab table. The muscles in his shoulders had bunched at the thought of what being in touch with Zoe Aberdeen meant. She was the type of woman who made a man lose his common sense but gain a thousand physical sensations that more than compensated.

"Yeah, we'll be in touch," he said hoarsely even though she was gone.

His eyes went to the beaker. He didn't believe in lust potions for one second, but he *was* tantalized by her invitation to misbehave.

Besides, she'd called him *handsome.* He was tickled. Absurdly tickled. Even if she was only teasing, no woman had ever flirted with him quite so effectively.

4

LATER THAT DAY, Zoe rapped lightly on the open door of an office at the area precinct. "Detective Arroyo?" She walked into the detective's office with her hand out. "I'm Zoe Aberdeen. Ethan's friend from the paper."

"Yes, of course. He's mentioned you." Nicole Arroyo pushed aside her paperwork and sprang up from her desk chair. Her handshake was vigorous, making Zoe's bracelets clink together. "Good to meet you, Zoe. Call me Nicole."

"I will, if you promise not to believe anything Ethan has said about me." Zoe laughed. "Lies! All of it lies."

Nicole didn't respond with a riposte about the flirtatious Englishman as expected. She frowned and distractedly pushed a loose hank of dark hair behind her ear as she lowered herself into the swivel chair.

"Have a seat." Nicole waved at a hard wooden chair set in front of her desk. The small office was crowded with a utilitarian desk, a bookshelf and an overflowing trash can. Several commendations hung on the walls, but Zoe couldn't read them, even when she squinted. Her prescription sunglasses were perched jauntily at the top of her head because she'd been making googly eyes at the clerk who guarded the squad room. She should have sprung for laser surgery when her trust fund was flush. Another opportunity missed.

"So." The detective rested her hands atop the stack of paperwork. "You want to know about the lust potion."

"The clerk—" Zoe motioned toward the lobby of the police station "—laughed at me."

Nicole picked up a pen. "I'm not surprised. The investigation is quite a source of comedy around here."

"Yeah, I can imagine." The atmosphere in the squad room was ripe with machismo. Blatantly admiring eyes had followed Zoe across the room as she'd made her way to the detective's office. She'd enjoyed the attention, even put a little extra *boom* into her *wacka-boom-boom*, but dealing with the scrutiny on a daily basis would soon become a bore.

Perhaps that was why Nicole had adopted the severe look and no-nonsense attitude. Zoe considered the other woman for a moment. Nope. Not even a tight ponytail and the unflattering cut of a mannish blouse could completely hide Nicole Arroyo's exotic, curvaceous appeal. No wonder Ethan was gaga. In his own subdued and composed British way, of course.

"And I really do mean that I can *imagine*." Zoe smacked her lips as a hunky male detective passed by the open door. His massive shoulders were strapped by a leather shoulder holster with a vaguely S and M appeal. "In fact, I'd be imagining all sorts of fantasies if I worked here."

Nicole's gaze touched on Zoe's clingy tank top. "Not if you wanted to be taken seriously."

"Seriously?" Zoe said with a flippant air. "What's that?"

Nicole's eyes widened. "You're exactly as Ethan described."

"Ah—Ethan. Dear Ethan. I love him like a brother. Well, maybe a cousin. The kind of cousin who comes for a visit the summer you're thirteen and ugly and leaves you with a nagging longing for blue eyes and disheveled hair that not even Hugh Grant movie marathons can cure."

Nicole had been clicking the pen rapidly, over and over. With a little grin, she tossed it aside. "I know what you mean. He's very…distracting."

Shane's image popped into Zoe's head—serious, brooding, smoking-hot even when she'd made him steaming-mad. "A girl's got to have distractions."

Nicole leaned forward. "So what's your interest in the lust potion?"

Zoe took out her notebook. She flicked through several pages filled with chicken scratches about designer dresses and drunken hookups. "What can you tell me about the investigation?"

"Not much."

"Because it's high security or because nothing's happening?"

The corners of Nicole's mouth twitched. "The latter."

"*Is* there an investigation?"

The detective swiveled to her computer and tapped at the keyboard. Zoe squinted as data flashed across the screen. Useless. If she was going to be an investigative reporter, she'd have to learn tricks like upside down speed reading. They hadn't taught a class like that at Amherst.

"Approximately six weeks ago, we sent a couple of officers to look into the allegations that this Jag person was ripping off tourists with a counterfeit lust potion while dealing the real stuff on the side. They returned with a sample, which we had analyzed."

"Oh, really?" Zoe tightened her lips. Why had Shane shoveled so much bull crap when he'd already done the analysis? "Can you tell me what the results were?"

Nicole hesitated briefly. "I don't see why not. The lab recently sent over their report." She struck another key. "The potion is harmless, ninety-four percent water thickened with an emulsifier, plus minor percentages of plant extracts—essential oils. There were also trace amounts of ephedrine, which would explain the minor tingling sensations reported by the dissatisfied customers."

Zoe's high hopes landed with a thud. She wanted to tell herself she hadn't expected otherwise, except that she had. "What about this tingling?" Kathryn had never called it *minor.* "Ephedrine is an amphetamine."

"Yes, but the lab report assures that because of the small amount present, the effects should be almost negligible."

"Nothing illegal, then? I guess that ends that."

Nicole nodded. "Basically Jag is selling doctored-up tap water for fifty bucks a pop. He's guilty of brazen huckstering, at best. The officers gave him a warning about the ephedrine and told him to cease and desist with the 'lust potion' claims. We haven't been able to nail down the allegations about a genuine potion. If he's dealing a second version, he's being very careful about it."

Zoe shrugged. "So much for *Balam K'am-bi,* the lust potion of the gods."

Nicole had pushed away from the computer. She made no response, simply studied the paperwork on her desk as if it contained the secrets of the Holy Grail.

Zoe knew she was missing something obvious. After a few seconds, she snapped to it.

"But there is the second sample," she said slowly. "The one that Jag planted in my bag. The analysis you've got there is of the sample taken by the officers when they raided the shop. Isn't that correct?"

Nicole went still. She said nothing.

"So *my* sample has yet to be analyzed. Furthermore, it seems that the anecdotal evidence about that particular potion is quite convincing."

The detective raised her eyes. "Anecdotal?"

Zoe leaned forward with a naughty smile, being a girlfriend telling tales. "My friend Kathryn says that *Balam K'am-bi* works magnificently."

A rather unprofessional squeak flew from Nicole's mouth. "She's used it, too?"

Zoe only smiled.

Briefly Nicole threaded her fingers over her face. "What has Ethan told you?"

"He's been absolutely discreet. But I can read by your expression how you feel about him."

"My, uh—" Nicole swallowed, staring down at her

lowered hands. "Any feelings I might have for Ethan bear no connection to the lust potion."

Zoe didn't believe her for a second. But she did believe that Nicole and Ethan's relationship had developed beyond the gotta-have-you-naked stage. Kathryn and Coyote were on the same path.

"Hmm." Zoe tapped a fingernail on the edge of the desk. "There's an interesting question for my article. Does the lust potion elicit feelings of romantic love or is it strictly about sex?" She straightened, holding her pen poised above the notepad. "What's your opinion, Detective?"

Nicole glanced at the squad room. Despite the knowledge that glinted in her dark eyes, she shook her head with unalterable vehemence. "No comment."

"ZOE," DONOVAN SAID WITH a moan. Sleep had eluded him after he'd settled into bed for the night. Now the sounds of his pesky neighbor's arrival home had permanently chased away his chance at the usual solid eight hours.

He stared up at the ceiling. The residual irritation about her disruption was no match for the redheaded fantasies that had danced in his head since their encounter in his lab. If he got the chance to do it over again, he'd sworn to himself that he'd kiss her. He'd sweep her into his arms and kiss her as though it were the last frame of a movie. Only with no fade to the credits.

It was time to find out where kissing Zoe led.

He listened intently, having become fairly proficient at discerning the various levels and origins of her misadventures. There was the low-level annoyance of her typical evening at home—loud music or TV, ringing phones, pizza delivery, running in the stairwell, the shrieking laughter of friends stopping by. There were her parties—one long blast of noise pollution, frequently culminating in music and dancing in the street. Sometimes damage to the building, the landscaping, or even his car.

But worst of all were the quieter times, when she'd brought a man home. From the balcony that adjoined both apartments, Donovan had seen the flicker of candlelight through her curtains. Through their shared walls he'd heard the low music—when he was weak, he imagined Zoe doing a striptease. That was followed by the long silences—surely the wet, smacking sounds were also his imagination—then the masculine groans, the feminine sighs, the thumps of a headboard knocking against the wall.

Those were the nights that Donovan slept with a pillow over his head. Or didn't sleep at all. A couple of times, when she'd been seeing a long-haired marine biologist who yelped like a seal at the crucial moment, he'd even taken to going for bike rides along the Embarcadero at three in the morning.

He rose up on his elbows, straining to discern the sounds from the hallway outside his front door. A normal person didn't make that much noise unless they were moving in, but this was Zoe, the traveling circus.

And she was speaking to someone. Did she have a new lover?

Unbearable. Donovan gritted his teeth against the jealousy.

He had to know. He vaulted out of bed, so hell-bent he disregarded his robe and slippers and crossed the living room in nothing but a pair of cotton pajama bottoms.

Zoe's soprano rang out clearly when he pressed his ear to the front door. "I know you love me," she said in a kissy-kissy voice, turning her keys in the lock. "But don't be so eager. Let me get inside."

Donovan butted his head against the door, then winced at the resulting thud. *Crap*. If she'd heard, she'd know he was spying.

He put his eye to the peephole. Zoe *had* heard. She was standing in her doorway, holding the half-open door tight against herself while staring toward Donovan's apartment. "Shhh." She made a motion to her companion, who'd apparently entered the apartment before her. "It's Mr. Cranky. We have to be quiet."

Then she didn't move or speak. Only watched his door.

Mr. Cranky stopped breathing. He pulled his eye away from the peephole. He lifted his left foot and widened his stance so she wouldn't see a shadow through the narrow crack at the bottom of the door.

Mr. Cranky was acting like a child, not a grown man. If he wanted to talk to Zoe, he should damn well open the door and—

Bing-bong.

He didn't wait a decent interval, only threw open the door before she rang again. "Good evening, Zoe." He glanced at his wrist. Bare. His watch was laid out on the bureau, with his wallet and keys. "Or morning, as the case may be."

Her open mouth snapped shut. She swallowed and said only a thin "Hello, Shane," while staring at his naked chest.

His nipples beaded. He resisted the urge to flex, wishing that he'd taken up sunbathing like Zoe, except that everyone knew sun wasn't good for your skin. Especially as a redhead, Zoe should—

Her chin poked out. "You're spying on me?"

"You woke me up, arriving with so much clatter."

"That's Santa, isn't it?"

"The reindeer, I think."

Zoe waved her hand. "So I dropped the dog dish. It's not even midnight."

"It's past one o'clock." Donovan checked his wrist again. Habit. "A dog dish?" he asked, distracted.

"I'm taking care of Falcon for the Valentines."

"They have a falcon?" he said in disbelief. At the same moment he realized that the scratching and whimpering behind Zoe's door was the Valentines' pet, not an eager suitor. Her men tended to thump and yodel like Tarzan.

"Falcon is a dog. A Maltese. I didn't want him staying alone, so I brought his stuff upstairs."

"But he's been alone the entire evening." Zoe hadn't come home after work. Not that he'd been paying attention, even though he'd skipped going out for beer with the usual gang of lab rats so he could get home early. In case she happened to be around.

"Shows what you know. I stopped by this afternoon

after my appointment at the police station and picked up Falcon. He's been riding shotgun all evening—and loving it."

The police station: A qualm niggled deep inside Donovan. "I could have let him outside, if I'd known the Valentines weren't home."

Zoe looked at him accusingly. "You'd have known if you'd come to my barbecue last Sunday. That was when Sara got the call that her dad had a heart attack."

Sara and Hailey Valentine were the mother-daughter pair who rented one of the ground-floor apartments. Nice people, even though the mother was always trying to fix him up with her divorced girlfriends, and the girl's teenage friends couldn't speak for giggling.

Donovan flushed. "About that. I—I was working."

He'd declined the backyard barbecue invitation because he'd felt embarrassed about the previous incident with the police. He'd imagined that Zoe would needle him for once again spoiling her party. Hiding out from his neighbors had been curmudgeonly, but he had too many memories of being the boy left out of the fun to put himself in similar situations even now.

Though Zoe wasn't one to nurse a grudge, she couldn't resist the chance to tease him. "Working on a Sunday, hmm? I suppose you were busy conducting chemistry experiments in the bathroom."

"I know how to make a stink bomb."

"Is that a threat?" Zoe laughed. "I bet you were the kind of boy who got only educational toys for Christmas."

She was right again, even if the only chemistry experiment he wanted to conduct these days included Zoe as the active ingredient. "How is Sara's dad?"

"Doing well after an emergency angioplasty. I talked to both her and Hailey a couple of hours ago. They'll be driving home from Palm Springs tomorrow. I want to do the neighborly thing and make them a casserole so they can have a hot meal when they get in. I just have to find a recipe. And some groceries."

Donovan was impressed by Zoe's thoughtfulness. Maybe she wasn't as flighty as she seemed. He briefly tried to imagine what kind of casserole she would concoct before deciding he'd rather not know. The cooking smells that came from her kitchen were unusual, but at least they were infrequent. At her backyard barbecues, she grilled anything that didn't move. Her standing pizza order was pineapple-jalapeño.

Sweet and hot and unconventional, that was Zoe Aberdeen. His complete opposite.

"Speaking of nourishment…" She leaned toward his door. "Do you have any food in your house?"

"Of course."

"My fridge is bare." She looked up at him, blinking hopefully. "And that sound you hear isn't the distant rumble of thunder," she added when he continued to hesitate. She pointed to her abdomen.

He looked down at the strip of flat stomach visible between her tank and the hip-bone-level waistband of her skirt. She *was* growling. "Not the dog either?"

"Connie doesn't growl. He's a sweetie pie."

"I've heard him barking when I take out my bike."

Donovan widened the door. "I can warm up some leftover Chinese if you want to come—"

"Love to!" Zoe darted back across the hall to collect the dog. Nestled in her arms, Falcon was small, white, decked out in a pink rhinestone collar—poor little guy—and twitching his whiskers at Donovan. She nudged the dog higher with her arm. "Go ahead, give him a pat. Make friends."

"I'm not an animal person." Donovan extended his hand.

"How come? Allergic?"

The dog's tongue flicked out, tickling Donovan's fingers. "No, I just never had a pet. They're a lot of fuss and bother, aren't they?" Full of germs, he was thinking, but he found himself scratching behind Connie's ears.

"Sure they are, but the unconditional love is worth it. I wish I could keep a pet, but at this point it's a challenge taking care of myself." Zoe snuggled with the little Maltese, her gaze slanting at Donovan. "But you seem like the responsible type. Want me to take you to the animal shelter and help you pick out a pooch?"

He withdrew. "I'll think about it."

Zoe spoke to the dog. "He says he'll think about it." She put Connie down, and the animal trotted over to sniff Donovan's feet. "Do you ever do anything without thinking about it first?"

He wriggled his toes. "I suppose not."

"Like grabbing a girl and kissing her?"

"What?" She'd startled him again. Had she been reading his mind? "Who? You?"

Her arms windmilled. "Anyone. Me, if you must."

His arms were leaden. He couldn't lift them. "That wouldn't be an impulse. I've thought about it too much."

"Logic rears its nitpicking head." Not at all put off by his confession, Zoe glanced around. His living room was furnished in a midcentury modern style of low couches and drum lampshades. He supposed all those rerun episodes of *The Dick Van Dyke Show* and *Leave It to Beaver* that his mother used to watch in the afternoons had had an unconscious influence on him when he'd gone to the furniture store.

"Where's the food?" Zoe said.

"Logic would say the kitchen."

Her smile was a beam of light as she sashayed past the open dining area he'd lined with bookcases that held an extensive collection of chemistry texts and potboiler mysteries. "Who knew you were such a smart-ass?"

"Hold on. I'll get my robe."

"Not on my account, I hope." She'd found the kitchen, switched on the light and was rummaging in his refrigerator. Connie had scuttled after her.

Donovan touched his chest. His skin felt so alive it jumped. Was Zoe actually expressing interest or was that all a part of her game? He remembered her mention an interview with the police. *Down, boy.* No need to go off half-cocked so soon.

Or fully cocked.

He shoved his arms into the terry-cloth robe he'd hung on the back of the bathroom door. There were slippers set out beside the bed, but he'd rather risk dog slobber than Zoe's amusement at his fussy ways.

Senses zinging, he went to the kitchen with his robe tightly belted, so she'd have to guess at his level of cockiness. She was eating a slice of bread spread with peanut butter and mustard.

"I can offer you something better than that."

"I'm sure you can." She chewed. "But MSG gives me a headache."

"How about something hot? It's December. The temperature drops even in Southern California."

She sat on one of the chrome old-time diner stools at his breakfast bar and crossed her legs, showing a lot of thigh. "I'm a New Englander by birth. This is like summer to me."

"I should have known from the accent." Traces of Katharine Hepburn playing cool and sophisticated slipped out when Zoe wasn't being her normal cheeky self. "How long have you been in San Diego?"

"Couple of years. Ever since I moved into this building."

He remembered that event well. She'd arrived with no furniture but three brawny moving men who'd announced several times that they were really actor/models. They'd carried up armfuls of colorful clothing in dry cleaner's shrouds, shoe boxes and enough expensive leather luggage to fill a cargo hold. The cases were so scuffed and scratched they looked as if they'd traveled the globe on the backs of skycaps, sherpas and possibly even elephants.

Zoe had gone around the building ringing door-bells and introducing herself. Before she'd even put her name on the mailbox, there'd been a party gearing up. Donovan had sat on the edge of a trunk as big as a crate, drinking a beer and watching Zoe take delivery of a pillow-top mattress and six pizzas while a cell phone was glued to her ear, then gone home with confusion and lust circling his head like honey-bees. He hadn't been entirely at ease ever since, even when he'd been seeing Victoria and was presumably less horny.

"How about you?" Zoe asked.

"I've been here since college, working in the same lab. I'm a creature of habit." Except that when he'd first arrived, he'd thought that he was breaking out of his rut by renewing the old ambitions of playing shoot-'em-up with the cops. While he knew in his gut that he was better suited where he was, talking to Zoe about it made him wonder.

"No family?"

"Dad died when I was fifteen." Resulting in his mother worrying even more over her only child, just when Donovan had needed to exercise his indepen-dence. He'd curbed himself, resorting back to books and daydreams, because he couldn't bear to cause any more grief. "My mother is still in the family home north of here. She has an older sister who lives with her now. They look after each other." Two widows fussing over coupons and canning the tomatoes. They seemed content.

He took out eggs, then loaded every green vegetable from his refrigerator to his arm. With the lifestyle Zoe led, she could use the extra protein and vitamins. "Why did you choose San Diego?"

"Fun in the sun, like everyone else." She licked peanut butter off a finger. The cap was left off the jar, the knife sticking out. "Plus, I had a connection at the *Times*. Anthony Tallant is a friend of a family friend."

"Who's Anthony Tallant? Remember, I don't run in your circles."

"My circles." Her voice went dull, until she crooned at Connie, who was dancing at her feet, his toenails clicking against the metal legs of the stool. "Tallant is the newspaper's publisher. And my circles aren't what they're cracked up to be," she said, watching Donovan tap eggs on the edge of a mixing bowl. "For instance, my circles have no food, outside of sprigs of lemongrass on snippets of salmon on slices of pumpernickel cut with a razor. A girl cannot live on hors d'oeuvres alone. I'm starving."

He chopped half a bag of spinach, then split and scraped the guts out of a pepper. He'd had enough of the bachelor life of pizza and beer with the boys during college, so he'd become workmanlike in the kitchen. But he lacked the flair to be a really good cook.

"How come there are no groceries in your house?" he asked, thinking that Zoe had flair to spare.

"I'm hardly home. No use keeping food when it'll only go bad."

"You can get it frozen or canned."

"I'd have to go to the supermarket for that. Besides, frozen food sucks."

Donovan's knife stilled over the sliced pepper. She'd sounded almost lonely. Was it possible that she wanted, even occasionally, the kind of companionship he craved?

Disregarding her penchant for odd food combinations, he ventured, "You probably have gourmet tastes, eating out at fancy parties all the time." *Tell me you value a good home-cooked meal, and I'll buy a Betty Crocker cookbook and study like I've never studied before.*

"Not as much as you'd think. Sometimes there's a lavish buffet, but often it's the same old finger food. Or Mexican takeout on the go. Should I mix the eggs," she said, not really a question because she was already vigorously wielding the whisk. The bowl filled with yellow froth. "You're being so nice to me, I almost forget..." She hunched, sounding sad again. Where her top sagged open, his gaze drifted to the cinnamon freckles sifted over her breasts.

Heat flared in his face. Hurriedly he switched on the gas burner of the stove.

"Forget what?" He'd never meant to become the grump of the building. It was his reaction to Zoe that made him surly. He'd focused on his disapproval of her slapdash lifestyle because he hadn't wanted to admit how much she turned him on. And now, how much he'd like to become friends with her, too.

She squinted an eye. "You're making me forget that I'm mad at you."

He hesitated, then plopped a pat of butter into a skillet. "Can you be mad at me later, after I've fed you?"

"How practical." She tugged on her straps, hiking up the tank an inch before he could glimpse one of her small pink nipples. "I can't switch off my emotions so easily. But I'm too tired to be fiery right now."

"Big night?"

"Nothing special. There was a rumor that Brangelina was in town with an entourage, so I hit the popular clubs. But my only brush with celebrity for the night was the Chargers quarterback, celebrating the latest win with twenty of his favorite teammates. He sent over a bottle of champagne."

"Sounds like your kind of guy."

She leaned her chin on her hand and let out a sigh. "The champagne was a bribe to get a mention in my column. You wouldn't believe what people will do to see themselves in print." Her eyes followed Donovan as he moved between the cutting board and the stove. Almost longingly. "It's not like he offered to feed me."

The dog pounced on a chunk of diced ham that fell as Donovan dumped the ingredients into the sizzling eggs. "Are you saying you prefer a practical-minded man?"

"Mmm, maybe. For balance. That yin-yang thing." She yawned and ran her hands through her hair, peeking at him through the tangled waves. "Objectively you and I might make a good match."

So she wasn't too tired to toy with him. "If you consider opposites a good match," he replied, telling himself to concentrate on stirring the eggs.

"Doesn't everyone?"

He dry-swallowed. "I tend to think that opposites would drive each other crazy."

"There's something to be said for the good kind of crazy. You need a little insanity in your life, Shane."

"I like my life the way it is," he insisted. But did he? He wasn't attracted to Zoe only because of her hot little bod. She was the free spirit that he'd never had a chance of being. She'd made him aware of how staid his own existence was and always had been. She'd made him remember.

The little boy who'd wanted to play tag with the other kids but wasn't allowed to and the young man who'd been rejected by the police academy had been buried deep.

But not deep enough.

Zoe dug into his green-eggs-and-ham dish with gusto. She chatted about her evaluation of the city's nightlife, including a rundown of the most popular DJs, the state of California politics, their landlord who refused to get a repairman to fix the balky water heater—everything but the lust potion and her visit to the police. By the time she'd helped Donovan rinse the few dishes and put them in the dishwasher, he was almost lulled into a sense of casual friendship, the kind of friendship she shared with everyone she met.

He could live with that. But it wasn't what he wanted.

They walked to the door. He was remembering his vow to kiss her—and her seeming encouragement—but she'd picked up Falcon and was giggling and shivering as he nuzzled her ear. Even dogs got more action than Donovan.

Zoe stopped at the door. "Well, thanks for the eggs. You were a life saver. I might have resorted to dill pickles and packets of hot sauce."

"You need someone to take care of you."

"No, I need to take care of myself." She straightened the buckle on the dog's collar. "You can teach me how to be a grown-up."

"It involves lots of paperwork."

She grinned. "And no more running with scissors."

"Anyway…" Donovan's gaze dropped. "You look all grown up to me."

Oh, man. What a cheesy line. She was within her rights to laugh at him for that one.

And she did, an openmouthed laugh that was warm and infectious, not you-are-such-a-bumblehead. "I'm surprised at you. I was sure I'm too skinny for your taste. Nothing like your last girlfriend, Dr. Victoria. Queen of support garments. I'll bet you had to duck rebounds taking off her bra."

"She never put an eye out."

"Too bad. You might look rather dashing in an eye patch."

He stepped closer. "You certainly do."

She blinked. "When have I worn an eye patch?"

"When you're sunbathing. But you don't wear it on your eye. I think you call it a bikini."

"Oh." Her irises had become liquid amber. "So you watch me?"

"I'm a guy, aren't I?"

"You are that." She squeezed the dog tighter. "Do you use binoculars?"

"No, but the guy next door does."

"Ew. He can see over the fence?"

"He goes up a ladder and pretends to be repairing his roof tiles."

"You might have warned me."

"I thought you liked the attention."

"It's my own backyard, with an eight-foot fence. I'm not an exhibitionist. I'm only..." She lifted a negligent shoulder.

"Uninhibited."

"Want me to teach you how?" Her voice lowered to a husky, coaxing whisper. "It involves *no* paperwork."

He put his hand on the shoulder she'd shrugged, where her freckles melted into the honey glow of her tan. For a woman so sharp—tongue, bones, wit—she had the softest skin and the warmest laugh. And the ripest lips, begging to be kissed.

As he bridged the gap between them, the rare sensation he'd experienced in the lab came back—the heady arousal of holding her close, an intoxicating desire to get even closer, the distant drumbeat of an urge to take her right then and there.

He *thought* he'd seen some of the same reaction in Zoe's eyes, but he hadn't trusted his ability to read her well enough to take the next step.

Go on. Do it. Step.

She turned her face up to his. Her lips parted. "Come a little closer."

His arms curved around her body. The dog squirmed between them.

Donovan didn't want to rush. Feeling the warmth of her was almost enough. Her sweet fragrance had developed undertones of musk. His fingers skimmed across creamy skin—her arm, her cheek.

She let out a breathy little sound, perhaps a sigh, maybe a moan. Either way, he took it as further encouragement.

Until she said, with the barest hint of testiness, "What are you waiting for? You do want to kiss me, don't you, even though I'm too skinny, too wild and my bad habits drive you crazy?"

"I…" His blood pounded. *"Yes."*

She wet her lips. Strands of her curly red hair teased his face like cobwebs when she turned away. "Then you shouldn't have lied."

He reared back. "What are you talking about? I said yes. I want to kiss you. I always have."

"I meant that you lied about the lust potion. I know you analyzed it."

"Oh, that." She brought it up *now?* He gathered his scattered brain cells. "I didn't lie. I haven't done a work-up of the sample that came from you and your friends. Wasn't that the one you were interested in?"

"Yes, but you knew I'd have liked to hear *any* of the results. Are you always so persnickety?"

"I told you—precision is a necessity in my line of work."

She held his gaze, her lips curved into an inscrutable Mona Lisa smile. While he had no idea what she thought of him, there was a distinct likelihood that she knew *everything* that was in his mind, fantasies and all. That might have made him self-conscious, but Zoe was the kind of woman who didn't shock easily.

"Detective Arroyo gave me the results," she said.

"Did she?" He didn't trust that Zoe wasn't fishing, trying to make him slip up and say more than he should. Maybe the way she'd encouraged the impending kiss had been calculated, too.

Except that he couldn't make himself believe she was cold and scheming, no matter how badly she wanted a story.

Whether there was a true—make that *mutual*—attraction between them was another matter.

"I gather it's not looking good for my sample," Zoe said.

Scientifically he was ninety-nine percent certain that the lust potion was a sham, but he didn't want to tell her that so bluntly when she'd been counting on writing an exposé.

"Probably not." He realized that he was still holding her by the shoulders and took away his hands, raising them like a wanted man. *Reach for the sky. Guilty of the crime of lust.* "I'm sorry to disappoint you."

Both of her straps had fallen off her shoulders. She held the dog nestled between her breasts. Falcon was *still* getting more action than Donovan.

Zoe turned to leave, but she stopped with one hand on the doorknob. "What I want to know," she said, looking back at him with her eyes like embers and her mouth like wild cherries, "is that if the lust potion *doesn't* work, how come I'm so hot for you now, when I wasn't before?"

5

"SHANE?" HIS FACE HAD changed, gone all stony San Jacinto on her—distant and unreachable. Zoe put Connie on the floor of the hallway, and he trotted off to sniff the edges of the terra-cotta tiles. "All I meant—"

"This isn't about the lust potion." Shane's jaw clenched. "For my part."

She'd screwed up. She'd thought he'd be thrilled to hear that she was hot for him, and instead he'd taken it as…an insult? Most men she knew couldn't care less why a woman wanted them, as long as she did. That Shane cared about her actual thoughts and feelings gave her a funny little shiver.

"No matter." Brusquely he tightened the belt of his robe. "I'll say good night now."

Zoe put her hand on the jamb so he couldn't close the door, even though the easiest thing would have been to let him go. The man wore a terry cloth robe. He kept a meticulous house. There were vegetables in his kitchen. He had—

Sex appeal. Unexpected but true.

She rocked forward on her clogs. "Please. I wasn't saying that I didn't want to kiss you."

"No, you were saying that you wanted to kiss me in spite of yourself. Because of an irresistible outside force—the lust potion."

"Let's think about that." She pushed up the strap of her top, her fingertips grazing the same skin that he'd touched. She could still feel his fingers like burn marks. Was that only a reaction caused by the potion? Could one small sniff have lasted for so long? According to Kathryn, her arousal had come from a more deliberate application.

"Is it possible that all this…" She moved her hand from her arm to his abdomen and felt the muscles flinch. Beneath the robe, his skin was hot. *Oh, my.* "That such a—a *strong* attraction is not real?"

"I don't believe in the lust potion," he said. "I can't state it any plainer than that. If you had no interest in me before and now suddenly you do, maybe you should take a look at your own motivations. Aside from notions of magical potions."

"Meaning it's all in my head, because I want the potion to be real?"

His expression was stubborn as he brushed her hand away. "Isn't that more likely than the potion being real?"

"There is another option." Boldly she widened his lapels and ran her palms over his bare chest, memorizing the contours as if he were a bas-relief map and she was lost. Delicious sensations careened upward through her veins, small shocks and sparks that kept her tingling even when she withdrew her hands. Lust potion or not, that was chemistry. That was real.

She rubbed her palms together. "I didn't intend to suggest that the lust potion was the only reason I feel this way. I was trying to say that I'm surprised my reaction to you could change so suddenly, without an impetus. A day ago, we were bickering about me not cleaning the barbecue grill, and now—"

Aha. She stopped and took a short breath. The penny had dropped, followed by another of the shivery thrills. "Okay, I get it. You believe that we've always felt this way, despite our disagreements. The potion has nothing to do with the fact that you want to, um, kiss my brains out and that I'm giddy at the prospect."

He gave her a speculative look. "That's right."

"So we're like Kate and Spencer, bickering opposites."

"Hepburn and Tracy? Us?"

She nodded. "The rule is that you always love the one you spar with—in clever, comedic ways, of course."

"If that's so, our banter needs a rewrite."

"Banter, schmanter." She pressed her knuckles hard into her thighs because she wanted to touch him again. "The point is that you think the potion has nothing to do with us and I think it was the catalyst, at least."

"No, the point is that you said before today you had no interest in me."

"Only because I wasn't looking as closely as I should have."

There was a drawn-out pause before he said, "I can accept that."

Her breath came short. "Which leaves us where?"

"Experimentation," he said and reached for her.

If she'd thought he'd be a tentative kisser, she was happily proved wrong. His kiss was a force to be reckoned with, a category-five tornado. Without any action of her own, she was lifted off her feet, propelled across the hallway and thrust against the door to her apartment. Hinges rattled. As did her brains. He really was going to kiss them out.

His mouth was the tumultuous center, a hot suctioning whirlpool that dragged her down into the depths of the kiss. There was no question of decision or even surrender. She was simply there.

And it was amazing.

Shane, she thought. *Shane, Shane, oh, great goodness, Shane.* Talk about hidden depths!

His hands were under her skirt, on her ass, hoisting her higher. She wrapped her legs around him, gripped his face between her hands. And kissed him. Kissed him back and front and in and out, until she didn't know which end was up or down or rubbed raw with desperation.

He kneaded her. She rode him, rocking hard against the pressure of his body, keeping her pinned to the door. The transition between then and now had been instantaneous. No chance to react with anything but instinct.

Her instinct was to go with it. All the way.

Shane had torn his mouth away from hers and was biting and sucking at her neck. Warm snorts of air fanned from his nostrils. She arched higher against him, her head thrown back in ecstasy, until she brought it around again, searching for his mouth, wanting the intense connection and the pure, deep pleasure of his kisses.

Connie started barking. An insistent *yip-yip-yip* that was bound to wake their neighbors.

"We have to...ooh, God...stop." Zoe slid like syrup down Shane's body.

He didn't let go, but his hands eased away from her hips, running up her back as he buried his face against her neck. A moan ripped loose, ragged and harsh.

"Whew." She tilted back and fanned her face. "I didn't know you had that in you." His unleashed desire had been overwhelming. Words seemed inadequate by comparison.

Shane couldn't answer for getting his breath back. Finally he disengaged and wiped his arm across his face. "Sorry. Did I hurt you?"

"Of course not," she said emphatically, even though she felt bruised and tender. "Don't be sorry. That was incredible. But is it possible you've been bottled up too long?"

He winced. "You may be right."

Seeing he was abashed, she grabbed a handful of terry cloth to keep him there. His belt had come untied. The robe hung open and loose against his body. The fullness of his cock beneath the pajama bottoms was evident. A shudder went through her as she remembered the feel of him like a molten iron bar against her belly.

She searched with one hand for the doorknob behind her. Why not invite him in? She could have him, have all that blazing, volcanic force inside her.

Zoe, the party girl, wouldn't hesitate.

Zoe, the last of the Aberdeens, did.

Her fist tightened, then released, letting him go. She closed her eyes to the sight of him, panting and lusty, his hair tousled and his face naked with desire, and made herself speak. "I think it's best if we say good night."

He nodded. "It's not best, at least not the way I'm feeling right now. But it's proper."

She gave a dry chuckle. "We zoomed past proper at a hundred miles per hour."

"Yeah, I…" Looking away, he wrapped the robe across his chest. "I don't know what got into me."

She knew exactly what had been a few caresses and a pair of dropped panties away from getting into *her.*

"Umm." She smirked. "Dare I say—"

"No, don't. This was obviously *not* a result of the lust potion."

Begrudgingly she had to admit that was true. Their chemical reaction had been all natural. Which only made her wonder how explosive the sex would be if enhanced by *Balam K'am-bi.*

But that wouldn't prove a thing as far as her questions about the potion's validity went. She'd been in a better position to test the concoction back when Shane was the uptight, annoying neighbor she'd had no thought of sleeping with.

Darn it. This wasn't the first time she'd been carried away by enthusiasm to the detriment of her goals. For once, she must keep in mind that she wanted to be taken seriously and work toward making that happen.

Shane appeared to have regained control. He'd backed off, and was staring down at his crossed arms.

She smoothed her skirt and hiked up her top. "I'm not giving up. If you won't help me, I'll find another way to learn the truth about the potion."

His jaw tightened. "Don't do anything stupid," he said, grounding out the words. "I'll help you."

"You'll give me the test results?"

"I don't know. I'll think about it. But I'll help you—somehow." He didn't seem happy about the prospect.

"Thanks."

He stared. "Was that why you kissed me?"

"Don't be insulting."

After a moment he said, "Right. That was rude. I'm just…" He shook his head.

"You need a little work on your social skills. Like maybe starting slower next time." She crossed the hall, laid her hands on his arms, went up on her toes and placed a quick kiss on his mouth. His lips were warm. "Good night, Shane."

He started to speak.

She stopped him. "Let's leave it at that."

His head bobbed in agreement. "Good night, Zoe."

With one last squeeze, she left him, turning to call to the dog before letting herself into the apartment, knowing beyond a doubt that Shane's confused face and driven kiss would stay with her all night, stealing her sleep. Good thing she didn't require the standard eight hours.

ZOE DIDN'T GO INTO THE office the next morning. Acquiring another bottle of *Balam K'am-bi* had become vital.

After taking care of Connie's morning walk and other needs, she hopped into her silver BMW Z3 convertible. The car was practically a cliché, but she'd bought it years ago on a whim for tooling around Southern California on her frequent visits. Now that she no longer had the funds to support a lavish lifestyle, the convertible was impractical to drive and expensive to maintain. She should have traded it in for a boring, reliable car. But in her business, appearance was everything. She was known around town, especially with doormen, valets and security guards—some of her primary sources—as the redhead in the silver BMW. She couldn't have flirted nearly as well out of a Dodge Dart.

The Gaslamp Quarter was the historic heart of the city's downtown area, a frequent hangout of Zoe's, with its hip coffeehouses, wine bars and nightclubs. The name had come from the old-fashioned gas lamps that had lit the quarter in the days of brothels and gambling halls. As always, the streets were packed with traffic, including pedicabs, trolleys and even horse-drawn carriages. The wide brick walkways jostled with pedestrians who ducked in and out of the funky shops and sidewalk cafés. Proprietors had decorated for the holiday season. The crowds were appropriately festive, even in the sandals and shorts that would never say Christmas to Zoe.

But that wasn't the fault of the warm weather. The holidays hadn't been the same for her since she'd lost her family. No ski lodge or beach hideaway could fill the void, even though the Aberdeens hadn't been the most traditional family. Her father had worked long hours as the chief neurosurgeon at Mass General. Her mother, a linguist who'd studied obscure dialects of Indian and African tribes, would rush in from a field study in Cameroon at the eleventh hour, apologizing that her gifts, invariably native-made art, weren't wrapped. Zoe's brother Rags—Reginald Aberdeen III—had been in medical research, and half the time they'd have to call him out of the lab for Christmas dinner. That, at least, had been traditional. Their treasured housekeeper, who'd been with the Aberdeens for three generations, tended to dip too frequently into the port and forget to follow recipes, but she'd always remembered how to roast a turkey and bake a gooseberry pie.

Zoe squeezed her lids shut behind her sunglasses. So what if her Christmases were no longer very Christmassy? That was the way she wanted them.

After circling the Quarter several times in the hopeless search for a metered space, she parked in one of the office building lots a couple of streets away from Jag's shop. She removed her heels, stuffed them into her bag, and slipped into a pair of flat huarache sandals, anticipating that her investigation might lead to back alleys or a hasty getaway.

She wandered the Quarter for twenty minutes before finding Jag's place again. Only a small placard identified his shop in a narrow storefront in a shabby Victorian on one of the less populated streets. The window was stuffed with colorful ethnic baubles and beads and other assorted junk.

She cupped her hands against the glass and peered

inside. The jumbled shop was badly lit by a flyspecked hanging fixture and a couple of dim sconces. A dusty palm overhung the window display, wanly clinging to life despite the lack of sunshine. Very little light reached past the shadow of a tall neighboring building and the lackluster awning that drooped over Jag's door.

A bell chimed as Zoe stepped inside. She hugged her bag even though the shop was empty. The place had seemed offbeat but harmless on her visit with Kath and Ethan. Now that she was suspicious of nefarious doings, she read the seedy atmosphere as creepy. Even menacing.

The same could be said of the little bald man known as Jag. With the sweep of a dingy curtain, he sidled out of a back room. Zoe looked up from the carved teak jungle cat she'd been eyeing, her usual cheery *ciao* dying on her lips.

Jag grinned, showing yellowed teeth. His beady black eyes crawled over her. "You looking for a little magic, huh?" So short he had to lift his arms to set his elbows on it, he leaned across the shop's main counter. Knobby brown fingers scuttled over the scarred wooden surface. "You want good times? Hot sex? I sell aphrodisiacs. Guaranteed arousal."

Zoe's skin prickled. "Do you have *Balam K'am-bi?*"

Jag's mouth and eyes became slits in his saddle-leather face. He made no response except to shake his head.

"The lust potion?" she persisted.

"No such thing."

"But you said—"

"There. Hot sex potions." He gestured at a nearby

shelf, where cheap bottles and tubes were packaged with claims of *Turn Her On!* and *Long-lasting Mount Vesuvius Erections!*

Zoe made a quick perusal. No sign of anything resembling *Balam K'am-bi,* lust potion of the gods. Even the small glass vials of the counterfeit concoction were gone, replaced with something called Lover's Revenge. She might have believed that the police crackdown had worked if greed hadn't clung to the shopkeeper's aura like sleazy massage oil.

She pretended interest in something called He-Man Spray. A basket of scrolls caught her eye, each no longer than six inches. A hand-lettered note card read *Recipes for Love.* Ninety-nine cents. She grabbed one labeled Lust Potion #9 and brought it to the counter. "I'll take this."

Jag rang up the purchase while she emptied the change compartment of her wallet. Great planning. If he insisted on cash, she couldn't buy the lust potion even if he offered.

"What happened to the *Balam K'am-bi?*" she asked, trying to sound casual. Clearly an interview was impossible. She'd have to wing it, encouraging conversation that might offer her some useful information.

"Never heard of it." Jag scowled. "You're at the wrong place."

She looked him in the eye. "I know it works. I was hoping to buy a bottle. Cash, of course."

Jag studied her, rightfully perplexed by the ninety-nine cents she'd counted out of her designer bag. "You've been here before."

She tucked the scroll away. "Once or twice. A friend told me about the lust potion."

The little man's face darkened. "No. It was you...."

Zoe was uncertain. Should she run? Or try to make a connection?

Real journalists didn't run. Besides, what could happen? Other than kidnapping, drugging and white slavery.

Telling herself that was ridiculous, she held her ground. "What do you mean? What was me?"

Jag's eyes were accusing, but his lips folded into a thin seam. He was giving nothing away.

"I'm not here to make trouble. All I want is more of the *Balam K'am-bi*. The *real* stuff. My boyfriend...well, you know. He loves it." She tittered, shaking her boobs like a bimbo nympho. "I can pay full price."

Jag's gleaming bald head snaked forward. "Five hundred," he whispered.

"Five...?" Damn. Double the rumored price from a few months ago. She calculated her MasterCard charges in her head, hoping there was room under her limit. "Do you take credit cards?"

"Cash only."

Double damn.

"How about a check?" Her paycheck was due today; she'd be able to cover the five hundred, pay the rent and still buy groceries. Barely.

"Cash only. No exceptions."

"I don't have the cash on me. I'll have to come back." She simpered and added perkily, in an attempt at deflecting his suspicion, "Gee, I guess it's lucky that we didn't use up the entire bottle yet!"

She turned to go, her mind whirling, uncertain whether she should take a chance and plunge ahead with the explanation that it had been her bag Jag had used as his drop. If he knew the "hot" vial had been turned over to the police, he might clam up.

His crackly voice stopped her at the door. "Wait."

She glued on a Barbie-doll smile. "Yes?"

"Write the check." With his head pulled low on hunched shoulders, Jag hurried off to the back room.

Zoe took out her checkbook. "Who do I make it out to?" she asked when Jag returned with a small brown paper bag. Having his full name would be helpful.

"Jag's. Like the sign says."

As she scribbled out the name and amount, she began to wonder why he was making an exception to the cash-only policy. Was the money enough to risk further interest by the cops?

She ripped out the check but hesitated before handing it over. A canceled five-hundred-dollar check would be evidence against him. Not ironclad proof of wrong-doing, but the first step in a paper trail. Jag's motives confounded her.

They made the exchange. Zoe took a quick peek into the bag. "This had better be the real potion."

Jag folded the check without looking at it. Odd—he seemed the type to count every penny. Furtively the paper was slipped into his pants pocket. "You get what you want. Hot sex. Multiple orgasms."

"Can I buy more of this when I need it? I have lots of friends."

Jag leered. "Orgies?"

She made a kiss with her lips, recoiling inside. "Maybe. We like to have a good time. And they're all big spenders."

He turned curt. "Rare potion. Limited quantities."

"Of course. It's sooo effective!" She shimmied her shoulders again, as if reliving the arousal. "What's it made of?"

Jag's gaze slithered toward the door as a bicyclist rode by. "That's a secret."

"Can't you give me a hint?"

"I could. Then I'd have to kill you." He cackled.

The line was so old it was moldy, but the cold glint of his eyes gave her a chill. She tucked the potion deep in her purse. "Uh, thanks, but I'll pass."

The urge to get out of the shop was strong. She risked one more poke at the sleeping bear. "There are rumors the lust potion is illegal. That the police are after you."

Jag sneered. "They know nothing. *Nothing.*" His eyes narrowed. "But you…"

Uh-oh. "I only want a supplier," she said hastily.

Even if he'd recognized her as his dupe from the day of the police raid, she hoped he'd assume that she'd returned because she was hooked on the potion's sexual exhilaration.

But if he was suspicious, he had her name. From the check. Worse, it was a recognizable name to anyone who read the *Times.*

Zoe thought quickly, albeit a bit too late. Thank goodness for her party-girl reputation and the loose morals of the fast crowd she reported on. That might save her.

She clamped her lips shut and motioned the turning of a key. "The secret's safe with me. As long as I can keep pleasing my man."

Jag muttered but seemed inclined to believe her. Or at least not ready to accuse her.

With one last flutter of her lashes, she scooted out the door while the getting was good.

6

Zoe waved at Kathryn, who was on the phone in her office. She thumped her chest and flashed hand signals like a Special Ops soldier on a mission, then slunk through the maze of cubicles to the break room. They could have huddled at her desk for a confab, but the corkboard walls had ears.

"Cripes, I'm hungry," Zoe said to the empty room. It was utilitarian at best, with a minimal kitchen area, a few cheap laminate tables and molded-plastic chairs scarred by the staff's attempt at office Olympics. One of the summer interns had torn a knee ligament hurdling them.

She threw open the fridge to see what she could swipe. A few of the newspaper employees had stashed brown-bag lunches inside. The remainder of the contents were not appealing: coffee creamer, an opened package of raisin English muffins that had turned into disks pitted with stones, brown-spotted fruit. She wasn't hungry enough to eat around the mushy areas.

Kathryn came into the break room as Zoe spied a blueberry yogurt. "Carbon-dating the fridge again?"

"Is November twenty-six edible?"

"You could risk it."

Zoe squinted at the sell-by date. *Nov. 26 05.* "Maybe not."

She returned to rummaging. "Why is there never anything to eat in this fridge?"

"Check the cupboards. I saw a package of cookies hidden behind that jumbo pack of Styrofoam cups." Normally all nonperishable snacks were secreted in the employees' desks, safe from the scavenging hordes.

Zoe pounced. Amaretto Milanos. "Success."

"When's the last time you ate?" Kathryn took a bottled water from the fridge. "Lunch yesterday?"

"Nope," Zoe said through a mouthful of cookies. She swallowed. "Last night. A spinach scramble. Shane fed me."

"Shane?" Kathryn dropped the bottle's screw top and it rolled under the table. She didn't retrieve it. "Your neighbor, Shane? The one you said is a hopeless dweeb? A tight-ass of the first order?"

"Not so hopeless. And not so dweeby." Zoe checked the counter surface for sticky stains, then hopped up to sit. She could watch the door from there. "His butt's still clenched tight enough to make diamonds from charcoal, but there are side benefits to firm glutes. Something to wrap your legs around, you know?"

Kathryn looked amused but not mystified. She did know.

Zoe stuck her nose into the cookie bag and shook it. She inhaled. The sweet fumes were almost as orgasmic as that first wild kiss with Shane.

Kathryn swigged the water. "Spill."

"Actually, that's not what I wanted to talk about. But if you insist…" Zoe stole a look at the door, then lowered her voice, even though her wild adventures were well bandied about the newsroom. "Shane works in the police crime lab. I went to him about the lust potion."

"Oh, Zoe."

"What do you mean, Oh, Zoe?"

Kathryn put on her scolding-schoolmarm face. "Did you boink him for a story?"

Zoe grinned. She'd often teased the formerly uptight Kath about how far she'd go to get a story, but beneath the banter they both knew that Zoe was more flirtation than follow-through. "Not so far. We stopped short of actual boinking."

"He didn't want to?" Kathryn said in disbelief.

Zoe didn't need to ask why that was the assumption. Even Kathryn was prone to assuming that in any given situation Zoe was the instigator, the cutup or the guilty party. Ninety-eight percent of the time, she'd be right.

"*I* didn't want to. Or maybe it was a mutual thing. We both recognized that we got a little carried away."

"You said he's not your type."

"He's not. He reminds me of my brother and father. Too brainy. Too literal. Too rigid." Zoe swung her legs, remembering Shane in the hallway, all heated up. "Maybe not *too* rigid."

"So you made out with him for a story?"

"The making out had nothing to do with the story. Unless it happened because of the lust potion, that is."

"*What?*"

"Shhh." Zoe brushed cookie crumbs off her skirt, a crinkled chiffon hippie-chic number. "Shane had a sample of the potion in his lab and I took a whiff." She pinched two fingers together. "A teeny tiny little whiff. Did you ever feel an effect from only a sniff of the stuff?"

"Uh…"

Zoe waved her off. "Never mind. I don't want the details yet. I need to experiment without any preconceived notions."

Kathryn sat at the table across the room. "Experiment?" she said warily.

"Before I can write a story, I've got to find out if there *is* a story."

Kathryn grew speculative. "What did the analysis say?"

"Shane wouldn't tell me. But Nicole Arroyo did. The potion the police recovered during their raid was, as rumored, bogus. The thing I want to know is if there's a genuine article to counterfeit."

She put down the cookie bag and rummaged in the carryall she'd slung crossways over her chest. "So that's why I went back to Jag's this morning."

Kathryn leaned forward with her fingers laced around the top kneecap of her crossed legs.

"And bought this." Triumphantly Zoe pulled out the bottle of lust potion. It was the same type as the first one, clear glass, rounded. No label. "Cost me five hundred bucks I don't have."

Kathryn stared, her eyes as bright and inquisitive as a squirrel's. Her knuckles slowly turned white. "Huh. That's a full bottle."

"Yep." Zoe tilted it back and forth so the fluorescent lights caught the rosy sparkle of the liquid.

"How do you know Jag didn't rip you off?"

"I had to take the chance. He was cagey about selling it to me. He refused at first." The deal with the check bothered her. Jag may have only agreed to the sale so he could get her name and address. But why? The potion might be evidence, but she'd made no hint that she'd gone—or would go—to the police. Even if she had, they'd shown no great inclination to arrest Jag or even close down his business.

Kathryn said, "I would think that he'd have shut down operations while the heat was on."

"But the heat isn't on, not to any high degree. Even though Shane still has the second sample, the police aren't begging him to run an analysis." Zoe shrugged. "I figure that's why Jag risked the sale at double the usual price." She weighed the small bottle in her palm. "Five hundred bucks? This stuff should be liquid gold."

Kathryn toyed with her pearl earring. Her gaze hadn't shifted from the bottle. "Maybe it is."

"The easiest way to find out is to test it."

"How? Or should I ask on whom?"

Zoe stirred with anticipation. "That depends, I suppose. I could shake out a drop and touch it to a passing stranger. Or, better yet, someone I can observe. Like one of our colleagues." She laughed at the havoc she might create.

"You already did that." Kathryn had been the unintended victim when they'd first found the potion in Zoe's bag and she'd playfully dabbed it on her friend.

"You've got to be more careful this time. Try it in a controlled environment."

"A controlled environment. Ugh. What's the fun in that?"

"There'll be plenty." Kathryn nodded. "Trust me."

Zoe wagged the bottle at her. "You and Coyote need a refill?"

"We're doing just fine without it." Kathryn's brows went up. "But if you're offering…"

Zoe kept silent while a coworker entered, filled a cup of coffee and asked them if they were "hardly working" before departing to stilted laughter. Once it was safe, she gave Kathryn a coy wink. "You'd have to give me a full report. All the juicy details."

"For publication?" Kathryn was appalled. "Not me."

"Don't be so hasty." Zoe chuckled. "You're not as conservative as you used to be."

"I think *you* need to try the potion. Then you'll understand."

"I plan to." Zoe mused over the bottle as she rolled it in her palm, her thoughts going to Shane. Her offer to be his guinea pig. The beginnings of attraction in the lab. Their explosive kiss. "But I want to be sure that I'm smart about how I approach this."

Realistically Shane was no longer an objective candidate. Yet she didn't relish the idea of dousing herself and a random stranger or acquaintance for whom she had no feelings, just to verify that the potion worked. If she was going to have hot jungle love, she was going to have it with Shane.

Kathryn stared, blinking. "Zoe? I *am* talking to Zoe Aberdeen, aren't I?"

She sighed. "It's me."

One of the newsroom assistants looked into the room. "Zoe, Bitterman's screeching for you." She came closer. "What's that you've got?"

"Perfume." Zoe tucked away the bottle and slid off the counter.

"Don't you wear Forbidden? That wasn't Forbidden."

"I'm trying a new scent."

The assistant sniffed. "I don't smell anything except calories." She looked at the cookie bag with disdain and smoothed her Lycra miniskirt over shapely hips.

"Not to worry." Zoe grinned at Kathryn. "I've discovered a great way to burn through them."

The young woman looked interested. "Want to fill me in?"

"Sure. When you least expect it." Imagining the stylish young woman hooking up with a JCPenney-clad fact-checker while under the influence of the lust potion would carry Zoe straight through the dreaded meeting with their managing editor.

"Don't you dare," whispered Kathryn as she slipped by.

Zoe laughed under her breath. "Oh, but think of the havoc I could create." If *Balam K'am-bi* was the lust potion of the gods, then she'd just become the high priestess of sexual chemistry.

"WHAT ARE YOU WORKING ON, boss?"

Donovan jumped. He'd been so involved he hadn't

realized that Guillermo was looking over his shoulder. "I'm about to run a chemical analysis."

"Can I watch?"

"Would you like to help?"

"Sure."

Donovan was careful about what he let the intern do. This case—a straightforward analysis of the second sample of a harmless fictional lust potion—was a good teaching opportunity. No vital evidence was at risk.

But of course he'd use every precaution all the same.

"Put on goggles and gloves." While Gil obeyed, Shane uncapped the sample that he'd previously freeze-dried by storing it in their freezer, which dry ice kept at a frigid minus-seventy-eight degrees centigrade. The sample was now back to room temperature.

"This was a liquid sample, originally ninety-four percent water. I've already rotovapped it." The rotary evaporator was a vacuumlike device that sucked the water from a sample. "Now we'll run it through the LC/MS. Get a syringe. You can inject the sample."

Gil opened the syringe packet. "What is that stuff, boss?"

Donovan didn't want to answer. It was too ridiculous.

He frowned. "A, uh, love potion." That sounded infinitesimally better than *lust*. Scientifically speaking. Personally he was all for lust.

Gil guffawed. "You're kidding me."

"Nope."

The intern shot him a suspicious look. "Is this a

hazing thing? Like how they send a rookie baseball player for the key to the batter's box."

Donovan pretended to be concentrating. With no answer, Gil would assume he'd guessed right and perhaps ask no more questions for. which he had no answer. "Inject the sample into the tube."

Gil worked the syringe, sending the sample into the liquid chromatography–mass spectrometry machine, or LC/MS for short. "Where'd we get a love potion anyway?"

"The police nabbed it from some huckster who was selling it in the Gaslamp Quarter."

"How does it work? The potion, I mean?"

"It doesn't," Donovan said. "It *can't*. We're proving it."

"But…" Gil's feet shuffled.

"What is it?"

"Aren't we supposed to be objective? If you go in planning to disprove—"

"You're right, of course." Donovan cut off the intern, stung by the innocent reproach. Maintaining impartiality was something he'd learned in Chemistry 101 and had wrongfully disregarded.

Zoe. She'd messed with his head.

He wasn't himself. And that was damn exhilarating.

Donovan continued with the analysis, sitting Guillermo in front of the computer screen as their results came up. There would be further results that would take longer to achieve, such as isolating the various chemical components, but for now they read the peaks on the graph that tellingly measured the sample's mass.

"Let's see what we've got."

"Ephedrine," Gil said, excited by the "discovery."

"That's interesting." Donovan leaned in for a closer look, suddenly feeling uneasy. "This sample differs from the first. There's another component."

"Cool."

"Let me get in here to see better."

Gil stood and pulled off his rubber gloves using the procedure Donovan had taught him—rolling them off inside out so no part of the exposed material would touch his skin. One of the gloves snapped back against his knuckles. Hurriedly he tossed the pair in the waste receptacle. "What is it?"

"Looks like…" Donovan pulled back. He frowned. "We may want to do an NMR." Nuclear magnetic resonance. "But it appears to be an animal pheromone."

BARBARA BITTERMAN LIKED TO intimidate even when she was having a cozy chat with one of her columnists. She sat on the edge of her desk, four inches too close and looming over Zoe like a gargoyle. Her unlined face, carved by L.A.'s top plastic surgeon, was immobile even when she smiled.

"Tell me what you're working on," she said, her silver-blond pageboy swinging forward around her face as she bent toward Zoe. "What's the hot gossip?"

"Christina Aguilera was spotted at Café Sevilla with a man who was not her husband." A waiter had called Zoe's cell with the tip. She'd zipped off in her convertible, only to find a bleached-blond look-alike who'd squeezed her size-four butt into size-zero hot pants.

Tracking pop tarts and their lesser-talented ilk was one part of Zoe's job that had started out exciting and soon become tedious.

Bitterman sniffed, her posture board-straight. "Empty calories. Give me substance."

Substance? From a gossip columnist? Zoe cast about her mental BlackBerry. "There's the upcoming singles' auction to benefit children with leukemia—"

"No, no, enough with the sick children. I want something fresh. Shocking. Let's turn this city on its ear."

"Yes, let's," Zoe murmured with no real conviction. Her enthusiasm for the job had been waning for a while, but it wasn't until being put on the spot by the family friends had forced her eyes open that she'd been willing to admit it. Now she had Shane, too. She wanted to live up to his standards.

"When Anthony persuaded me to hire you, he said you'd bring a new demographic to our stodgy readership. Hip, young, sexy." Bitterman whipped a copy of the day's paper off her desk. She brandished the page with Zoe's latest column under her nose. The smell of ink and newsprint wafted in the air. "Champagne with the symphony, Zoe? 'Mrs. Kellington wore vintage blue Dior.' That is neither hip nor young nor sexy."

Zoe clenched her hands in her lap. "I'm working on a story. I think it could be a blockbuster."

The managing editor stared loftily. "Yes?"

"There's a new fad. Sort of a, uh, drug."

"Crystal-meth addicts are not sexy, even when they're celebrities."

"It's a lust potion."

Bitterman laughed without true amusement. "Really. That's quite creative, Zoe, but there must be some truth to your fictions if they are to be believed by Mr. and Mrs. Average over their morning coffee."

Zoe started counting to ten. She stopped at six. "It's called *Balam K'am-bi*. It comes from the Yucatan. I'm surprised you haven't heard. Everyone's using it, even the symphony crowd."

At the barb, Bitterman checked herself as she made her way around the immense desk with her back to Zoe. She recovered smoothly and eased into the leather chair she'd hiked up to throne level. If she'd been an actual gargoyle, her arch expression would have turned Zoe to stone. "Is that so?" she said in a voice like the Mojave. "What was the name again? *Balam...?*"

"*Balam K'am-bi*. It's quite the rave."

"A lust potion, you say."

"Yes."

"You can verify its existence." Not *can you*. Barbie preferred issuing orders to asking questions.

"I have a sample," Zoe said rashly.

"Then you've tried it yourself."

"Not yet. I'm working on it."

"I can't imagine why there should be a delay," the editor said. She manipulated the touch pad of her computer with a finger that bore a walnut-size diamond, not bothering to maintain eye contact. "You're an active young woman." Her tone had taken on the slightest hint of disapproval. "I imagine you're game for almost anything."

"Research comes first," Zoe said, confronting the woman with a level stare. If the editrix asked her outright to hook up for the *Times,* all that teasing she'd done with Kathryn about boinking for a story would seem as funny as a funeral.

The editor stopped short of that, but she looked annoyed. "What is this potion? Liquid Viagra?"

Zoe supposed that Ms. Bitterman might have experience in that area. The rumor was that she'd once been involved with their publisher, Anthony Tallant, and he was a suave sixty, an Ivy Leaguer with a George Hamilton tan who was working on his third or possibly fourth marriage.

"Something like that," Zoe said, "except that it works on women, too. I'll get the chemical analysis very soon and then I'll know more." She planned to send some of her new sample to a commercial lab, as Shane had suggested.

"Hmm, and where is this sample you've acquired?" Bitterman's bored tone belied the sharp interest in her eyes when she glanced away from the screen of the sleek laptop.

Zoe took her time and answered with a half-truth. "Like I said, it's being analyzed." Even though the prospect of a full reimbursement for the cost of the latest bottle was appealing, she was *not* turning over the potion until she had a good idea of where the story stood.

Bitterman's lips thinned, a sign of her concession. "The story sounds preposterous, but I suppose you may as well continue. At the least, it should be good for a few amusing tidbits in your column."

Zoe shifted, ready to spring up and away. "Yes."

"Keep me updated."

"Of course."

Bitterman flicked a finger toward the door. "Go on, then."

Zoe went, like a gazelle from the lioness.

7

ZOE SAT BEHIND THE WHEEL at the stoplight on Harbor Drive, feeling flush with anticipation. Her salary had been direct-deposited in her account that morning; she'd been able to cover the check to Jag and put cash in her pocket. She'd survived the meeting with Barbie the Editrix, even if the pressure was now on to produce. The sun was shining, the Pacific beckoned with an ultramarine allure and she was a redhead in sunglasses in a flashy silver convertible.

Her one problem was that she had lust on the brain.

Some problem!

Zoe's laugh caught the attention of a group of Navy sailors running toward the beach in formation. They whistled in appreciation and she waved, taking a moment to admire their strong brown legs in short shorts, until the honking behind her became too insistent to ignore.

While driving to Donovan's lab, she marveled at her temporary lapse into sensibility. True, there was nothing *wrong* with setting up a goal like turning the lust potion into her ticket to journalistic fame and fortune. Her folly had been in thinking she'd get there by neglecting the lessons of the past nine years.

She was not Zoe Egghead, the girl who'd skipped three grades and gone to college at sixteen. She was impulsive. She was reckless. She was wild.

She should not revert to the Aberdeen tendencies of planning and plodding. If she really wanted to succeed, she had to take risks.

In the parking lot, she waited for a group of technicians to leave before taking out the vial of lust potion. She didn't care to attract scientists at random. One specific nerd was enough.

A tremor broke inside her when she unscrewed the top of the bottle. She stopped and sucked air to the bottom of her lungs, trying to steady herself. But the anticipation was too much. If the stories were true, sensual decadence awaited inside this one small bottle. Adventurous, exciting, bedazzling sex.

Perhaps even love.

She wasn't actually *looking* for love, but finding some form of it wouldn't be objectionable. Along with her job dissatisfaction had been the growing feeling that maybe it was time to learn what it'd be like to have the kind of boyfriend who'd be there in the morning to bring in the paper and do Sudoku puzzles and read horoscopes—all right, maybe box scores—and share breakfast and a laundry basket.

Her thumb pressed to its mouth, she tipped the bottle. The liquid touched her skin, and immediately a second slithery tremor went through her. Whether that was of her own manufacture or a symptom of the potion, she couldn't tell. How did one ever know for certain?

She rubbed her barely wetted thumb against her index finger and brought them to her nose. There was a faint smell this time. Not as strong as perfume yet still a distinctive scent. She sniffed straight from the bottle.

Oh, yes. Spice and musk.

Zoe sat very still, waiting for the tantalizing arousal that was supposed to follow.

Nothing happened beyond the low humming elation that had already filled her veins.

A few more employees exited the building, a square, squat monolith of ochre stucco and steel-banded windows. Sunlight filtered through a row of tall palms planted behind a concrete wall. It was quitting time. She'd timed her arrival to catch Shane in the lab without too many coworkers around to interrupt. But she couldn't delay for long. She needed to get into the building in order to get into it with Shane.

The sound of departing vehicles was a distraction. She closed her eyes, concentrating on her bodily functions, checking for the telltale signs. Her stomach was hollow. Her pulse raced. And when she thought of Shane, she became very aware of the shape of her lips and the tips of her breasts. Evidence of arousal, to be sure, but only applicable if she hadn't been experiencing them pre-lust potion. And she had. Ever since their kiss.

She needed incontrovertible proof.

"Let's give this another try." Zoe put her right finger over the bottle and dipped it again, letting a good dollop leak out. A rivulet trickled toward her knuckle. She swiped it across her wrist, then at the hollow of her throat, touching a fingertip to her lips for good measure.

She smacked. Yes. This was getting good. She felt a definite tingle. Not the overwhelming lust Kathryn had described but enough to work with considering she meant this to be a preliminary experiment, not an all-out boinkathon.

Time to rendezvous with Shane and see if he reacted, too.

Shane's young intern was hanging around the reception area, talking to the receptionist's cashmere-clad boobs. She—or they—seemed to be enjoying the attention.

"Guillermo," Zoe said, waving her hello to keep him at a distance. She intended to heed Kathryn's warning that the potion's effect was powerful and easily trans-ferable. No contact except with Shane.

"I'm here to see Donovan Shane," she said to the receptionist, walking while talking. "He's expecting me. Shall I go right up? I won't be staying. He's taking me out to, um, dinner. Right away."

"You can't—"

"Oh, yes, the visitor's badge. We mustn't forget that, right?"

"I suppose…" The receptionist fished in her desk. "You'll have to sign in. And I'd better call Dr. Shane to see if—"

"Oh, never mind that. I'll just zip in and say hello." Extracautious, Zoe used her left hand to inscribe a wobbly signature. She snatched up the visitor's pass and backed away. Guillermo had been leaning across the desk, his nostrils flared and his eyes hungry for more than a Quarter Pounder. Except he'd been focused on the receptionist, not her.

Zoe dashed away. She snipped a dangling thread of concern while flying up the steps to the second-floor lab. Guillermo was having a normal teenage male moment; nothing to do with the lust potion. He hadn't gotten a whiff.

All the same, she used her left hand on the door latch into Shane's lab so no trace of the potion was left behind. Who'd've thought? There might be some benefit to proceeding with caution and forethought like a true Aberdeen.

The lab was empty. She walked through and found Shane in the adjoining office, deep in contemplation, sitting behind a big metal desk stacked with thick books and piles of paperwork and files. His head was in his hands.

"Shane?" she asked, abandoning thoughts of making a sextacular entrance. "You okay?"

He looked up in surprise. "Zoe! I wasn't expecting you."

"I came on a whim."

He flushed and turned over the clipboard on his blotter, then compulsively checked his watch. "Visitors' hours are over."

"I told the receptionist that I wouldn't stay long." Zoe approached, her clammy palms glued to her hips. She hadn't been this nervous since her appearance in the National Spelling Bee. As long as Shane didn't ask her to spell *elegiacal*...

He stared, but she couldn't read his eyes. The wire-framed spectacles reflected the fluorescents overhead. His hair was already rumpled, and his hands twitched as if he wanted to run them through it once more. The desk chair creaked as he leaned back, tucking his hands against his ribs. "You've wasted your time. I have nothing to report."

"That's all right. I didn't come here for that." She stopped at the edge of the desk, waiting several awkward seconds for the potion fumes to reach him. Shane remained resolute, almost skeptical in the way he studied her.

She fluffed her hair and smiled hopefully. He didn't budge except to grunt and ask, "Then what do you want?"

"Oh, you know. Just to say hi. See if I can entice you…" She let her words trail off, but he didn't jump in with indecent proposals. "Entice you to go out for a drink."

"You're snooping."

"I swear I'm not." She stroked her collarbone, trying to get the potion's molecules dancing.

Shane took off his glasses and pinched his nose, watching her all the while. She felt ridiculous standing there like a lump. The potion wasn't working at all, and neither were her natural charms.

"Warm in here," she murmured, picking up a file folder and fanning her face. She needed him to come out from behind that desk and get a good whiff. Or a taste. Maybe the potion's full effect didn't work without actual contact.

"It's not that warm."

She laughed. "Then it must be your hotness that's getting to me."

He scratched his temple. "You're kidding, right?"

"Hmm." She circled the desk. "Just trying to keep the mood light. You seem tense." She reached for his shoulders. "I know Jin Shin Jitsu."

"What's that? A trendy form of karate?"

She put her mouth near his ear. "Kind of like massage, you big dolt." His shoulders got a big squeeze. She worked her thumbs against knotted muscle.

"Thanks, but..." He tried to rise.

She pushed him down. "Sit. Relax. Just for a minute." Long enough for the potion to rub off on him. "The receptionist calls you 'Dr.,'" she said to keep him occupied.

"That's just Mandy Rae being officious." He groaned a little in his throat. "I have a Ph.D. in chemistry, but I don't introduce myself with the title. It puts people off."

"Not me," Zoe said. "My family was chock-full of Ph.Ds."

"Oh?"

"Never mind. They're gone now." She kneaded his firm flesh. "How come you're working here? With a Ph.D, you could have a research position with one of the big drug companies. There's a lot of moolah in research." Her brother Rags had raked it in, though he'd been too busy putting in endless hours at the lab to enjoy the income.

"Money's not that important to me."

"Me neither. Except when I'm broke."

"Come on. I've seen your car and your wardrobe. You're not broke."

"Only when I'm between trust fund payouts," she fudged. Her new accountant had put the remaining money into safe investments that would grow slowly but steadily over time. Feeling guilty over her profligate years, she hadn't withdrawn a penny since moving to San Diego, even when she had to resort to grazing on hors d'oeuvres.

"But you didn't answer my question. Why the police crime lab?" Under the guise of stroking toward the front of his shoulders and upper chest, she rubbed her wrist against Shane's jaw. Surely he was feeling something by now.

He stretched his neck. "I'm a wannabe detective."

She went still for a moment before resuming the massage. He'd made the comment lightly, yet she'd heard the ring of truth to the words.

Even so, she chuckled. "Been watching too much *CSI?*"

"That must be it." He shrugged away her hands. "Enough massage. Uh, thanks."

Impulsively she bent to hug him loosely around the shoulders. Her lips grazed his ear, his cheek. "You'd make a great detective. All those details requiring a meticulous mind."

Shane stiffened and tried to turn to look at her, but she wouldn't let him out of her embrace. "So now I'm *Monk?*"

She patted his chest. "Not that bad."

The potion was a dud. She'd rubbed it all over him. He should be kissing her by now.

Instead he reared his head back to look at her with his face pulled into skeptical frown lines. "What are you doing?"

She stepped away. Batted oh-so-innocent lashes. "Being friendly?"

"Last night," he started, before stopping to rub his jaw and tug his collar. "Last night…"

"We kissed, Shane. That's all. It wasn't a proposal of marriage, so don't worry. I kiss lots of men." Although none of them quite so…so…memorably.

She swept up her long, swishy skirt and went to sit on the opposite side of the desk. She put her bag on her lap and rummaged through it, avoiding Shane's puzzled face, feeling rather puzzled herself. She'd assumed he was trying to put a distance between them and had meant to reassure him that he was under no obligation.

"Then that's fine," he said, although his expression was all wrong.

Her answering smile was distracted. At least the cooling between them was beneficial to her lust-potion experimentation. Which was, so far, a bust. Their attraction seemed to have flatlined.

"But you're not rid of me yet." Inside the purse, her hand closed around the bottle of *Balam K'am-bi*. She hadn't used enough, that was the problem.

Shane cleared his throat. "The thing is, I don't want to be rid of you."

She glanced up sharply. Was that the lust potion talking?

"I've had a—a crush, I guess you'd say. A crush on you. For a long time."

"Stop!" She flung up a hand. "I don't want to hear it." She dived back into the purse. Realizing that had sounded harsh, she said, busily uncapping the bottle, "What I mean is, can we save the secret confessions for later? After drinks, maybe dinner. When the mood is—oh, damn."

Shane rose halfway from his chair, trying to see what she was fiddling with. "What *are* you doing?"

The cap had suddenly come off, spilling the potion. She'd caught most of it in her palm, but she was dripping. "Do you have a tissue?" she begged, screwing the top back on and closing the bag just as he came around the desk to see.

He gave her a Handi Wipe from a packet on his desk. "What's that liquid?"

"I spilled perfume." She stood, mopping her hands before she brandished the wipe under his nose. "See? Smell."

He took the cloth, sniffing cautiously. "There is a scent. For a second there, I thought you were trying the potion on me. But it doesn't have an odor." His eyeglasses glinted. "And you *claimed* you don't have any more of it."

"Is that a question?" Her hands felt warm and tingly, which had to count for something.

"Will you answer it?"

She kept silent while waiting in vain for the potion to take further effect. A little tingling was fine, but where was the undeniable lust?

With a sinking sensation, she thought of the money she'd spent. Five hundred dollars.

"Zoe?"

She closed her eyes. *Grab me. Kiss me. Take me.*

"I was right," Shane said, unmoving.

"Yes." She sighed, her shoulders drooping as she gave up. "I went back to Jag's and bought a bottle of the lust potion." *Five hundred dollars!* "It doesn't work."

"I could have told you that."

Her head shot up. "Then you've analyzed it."

He stepped back. "I began the process."

She advanced. "And?"

Her hopes rose even higher as he hesitated, but when he finally answered, it was with conviction. "Believe me, Zoe. There's no way the potion is real."

"But people have told me—"

"All in their mind."

"They've *experienced* it," she insisted, knowing they'd had this discussion before. Shane stubbornly remained a man of logic and science. She believed—or at least wanted to—that there was magic in the world. "There have been actual physical reactions. That says more than a chemical analysis. Words on paper."

"It says only that the mind is a powerful tool. These people you mention felt what they wanted to feel." He rubbed the dampened wipe across his nose and chin. Flung open his arms. "You see? Nothing."

"Nothing?" She took his face in her hands and planted a big, juicy kiss on his parted lips. An electric charge zinged between them. "That was nothing?"

"No, Zoe, that was something." He brought his hands to her hips. The stubborn logic peeled away and she saw again his naked desire. Though he didn't know it yet, that force was ten times as strong and drew her to him as surely as iron filings to a magnet. "But it wasn't the lust potion."

She had to agree there. But she could be stubborn, too. "All right, maybe the bottle I bought this morning is the counterfeit potion." The weight of the carryall dragged at her shoulder. With her head butted against Shane's chest, she fumbled for the bottle, then let the strap slide away. The bag dropped.

He gave her hips a pat. "I'm sorry."

A moan slipped out, sounding something like surrender, but she kept the bottle clasped between them. "I feel like a fool, spending money I couldn't afford."

He wrapped her in a hug. She hugged him back, clumsily one-armed, then gave in and twined both arms around his neck. "But I won't give up." She sniffed. The smell of the fake potion was heavy in the air. Yet she recognized Shane's clean male scent beneath the layer of thick musk. She buried her face against his chest, inhaling him into every cell of her body.

"You have to," he said gently. "You're chasing a fantasy."

"I *can't* give up. This is my chance."

"For what?"

"To *do* something. To make my mark." Her voice was muffled. "I've wasted so much time."

"You'll find another story."

"No." She pushed away from him. Lifted her hair off her face with an air of defiance. "The lust potion is it. There's a story there. I can smell it!"

"You smell it, huh?"

She realized what she'd said and laughed a slightly maniacal laugh.

Shane's brows rose. He'd heard the edge of desperation, too.

Zoe saw herself through his eyes. A nutty nut nutball, blowing her cash on a wild scheme, all because a few people had gotten some hot sex and given her delusions of a grander life.

But she wasn't throwing in the towel. Not yet. She was certain that Jag was up to no good, one way or the other.

Zoe was drawing breath to explain herself to Shane when there was a knock at the door that opened to the hallway. It opened. "Dr. Shane? Are you busy?" The receptionist poked her head inside. "It's almost six."

"Mandy Rae. I'm sorry we've kept you. Go ahead and leave." Shane glanced at Zoe, and she thrilled at the light in his eyes and the hungry way he looked at her. "I'll be seeing Ms. Aberdeen out."

"Yes, sir." Mandy Rae's nose twitched.

Guillermo's face appeared over her shoulder. "What's that smell?"

"Perfume," Zoe said.

"Gil?" Shane asked. "I thought you left hours ago."

Gil's eyes went to the receptionist. He made a dopey smile. "I meant to."

Mandy Rae was still sniffing the air. "It's better than

the usual stink." She nudged the intern. "Guillermo? Weren't you taking me to In-N-Out Burger?" With a flip of a honey-colored ponytail and one last besotted grin, they were gone.

Shane frowned. "That's odd."

"What?" Zoe asked. "They're young and in love. I think it's cute."

"They weren't in love this morning. Besides, Mandy Rae is twenty-one. Do you know any twenty-one-year-olds who date high school presidents of the chemistry club?"

"Well, no."

"They must just be friends then."

"They didn't look like just friends to me." Zoe speculated. There was something off about Shane's reaction. For one, he wasn't the type of guy to gossip about—or probably even notice—an office flirtation between his minions. Two, why would he comment on this one in particular, to the point of calling it odd?

She gasped, seeing the obvious reason Shane might be concerned. "Does Guillermo have access to the lust potion?"

Shane scoffed. "You can't be thinking—" His teeth clicked together and he briskly shook his head. Denial was written across his face. "Impossible."

Denial as an answer…or denial as a refusal to admit she might be on to something? A surge of hope bolstered Zoe. "You were working on the potion today. Guillermo was here."

Shane crossed his arms. "Yes."

She smoothed his rumpled tie. "So it *is* possible that Gil may have decided to try the potion?"

"He may have. But he wouldn't. He's a good kid. Besides, it's not as if they were climbing all over each other, overcome with lust. They were only going out for burgers."

"True. But maybe he used a very small dose."

"Gil would *not*—"

"Ah, but what if he didn't realize?" Zoe became excited as she put the scenario together. "Think about it. Their reaction was mild. All it would take is a drop."

"We wear gloves. Coats. Protective eye wear."

"But it's possible."

He sighed. "Only if the potion was actually a potion and not water with a few chemicals and oils tossed in to pretty it up."

There was a slight touch of doubt in his expression, but instead of seizing on it, Zoe strode away from him, entering the lab. Her thoughts were in turmoil. When she realized the bottle was still in her hand, she slammed it down on the black surface of the lab table. She would break through Shane's refusal to see the possibilities. She whirled to face him as he followed her. "Prove it!"

He was taken aback. "What, you want me to analyze a new sample?"

"No, this bottle is counterfeit. I'm sure of that. I think…" She tapped her chin with a finger and got a renewed whiff of the fake potion's spicy fragrance. She remembered how she'd felt after sniffing straight from the beaker. The arousal had been brief but strong, resulting from the potion itself, not from a scent.

At the back of her brain she wondered. *Resulting from the potion…or the man?*

"Did the first sample you analyzed have a scent?" she asked Shane.

"I—I don't recall."

"Mr. Meticulous doesn't recall? I'm sure if you think about it, you'll remember."

He pushed up his glasses. "Yes, actually. It must have had a scent. There were essential oils in it, extracted from native South American plants."

"Aha! Suppose the counterfeit potions are all scented. You know, for show. It's only the real *Balam K'am-bi* that doesn't need the fancy dressing."

He hesitated for a nanosecond. "There is no real *Balam K'am-bi.*"

"So you say. Then why won't you prove it? Or let *me* prove it."

Shane walked across the room to the row of beakers and test tubes. "I can't give you the sample."

"Because of regulations? Or because you know—or you suspect—that I'm on to something?" She had to clench her hands and dig in her heels to stop herself from running after him and snatching away the beaker.

Shane tilted the glass container. The liquid pooled, shimmering slightly.

"Please, tell me what's in that potion," she pleaded.

"I'm still processing, but I will say that this sample was slightly different than the first."

Zoe's mouth opened. "Different how?"

He refused to answer. "I'm certain it isn't a vital difference."

"You're not certain." She could read that in his face and the implication was so momentous she could hardly breathe. "*Balam K'am-bi* is a real lust potion."

"It is not." The moment of uncertainty had passed and his face was set in stone. "There are obscure chemical ingredients, yes, but the potion is harmless. You could bathe in it without result. Pour it over your head. Drink it." He was positively glaring at her. "I promise you, Zoe. *Balam K'am-bi* is not a lust potion."

Much to her shock, he lifted the beaker to his mouth, tilted back his head and swallowed some of the potion.

Her world went into slow motion. She watched the slide of his Adam's apple, the smack of his lips, the slow turn of his body as he lowered the beaker to the table and swung around to confront her. His eyes blazed. His chest expanded as he took in a deep breath.

"You see?" he said. "No change. I'm exactly the same. Listen to me, Zoe. Really listen." She had no choice—his voice seemed thunderous in her ears. *"There is no such thing as a lust potion."*

8

DESPITE DONOVAN'S CAUTIOUS NATURE, he'd made a few blunders over the years. Backing up over the mailbox on the first day he'd had a license was bad, especially because his mother had been taking photos at the time and still liked to pull them out and play "Remember When." Participating in a fraternity slave auction had been a lousy idea, particularly when the bidding had topped out at three dollars and seventy-five cents from a musclehead jock who'd expected Donovan to take his Chem exam. Telling Dr. Victoria that she was making a mistake returning to a cheating husband—while she was dilating his eyes—had been worse. He'd worn the Ray Charles sunglasses for twenty-four hours.

But drinking evidence was the all-time worst.

He could lose his job.

He'd already lost his senses.

A wave of strong sensation rolled through him, as warm and buoyant as the Pacific in July, nearly lifting him off his feet. He staggered, then caught himself. He leaned against the lab bench, arms braced, elbows locked, battling for control. And hoping against hope that Zoe hadn't noticed.

"Oh, Shane." She rushed over to steady him. "Why did you do that?"

Dizzy. He put his head down. "I don't know."

"Are you all right? How much did you swallow?" She fluttered nervously. "Should I call Poison Control? Find a bottle of ipecac?"

"God, no. I'm okay." *I hope.* He gulped for oxygen. Suddenly the air seemed too cool against his hot skin and the tumult boiling up inside him. "I'm fine, I'm fine." His stomach churned. A wave washed over him. "Maybe a little light-headed."

"But we don't know what effect the potion will have. Especially ingested at that rate."

"It wasn't so much." He gestured at the beaker. A half inch of potion remained. "Only a mouthful."

"But when one drop is powerful, what's an entire mouthful going to do?" Zoe looked at him warily, as if she expected him to sprout an erection the size of the Eiffel Tower. "Are you already having symptoms?"

Let's see… His taste buds were doing a jitter bug. The power surge blitzing through his body could light all of Southern California. His heart was pumping molten lava. And it was quite possible his growing erection, while not yet epic proportions, would *sproing* free and bust out the zipper on his khakis.

So of course he said, "No."

"Then how come you're sweating?"

"I am sort of hot. It's the ephedrine." He tore off his lab coat and let it drop to the floor, trying not to look at her, because if he did…

She was studying him. "What does it feel like?"

He closed his eyes. The insides of his lids were fiery red, punctuated with bursting black stars. That wasn't normal. He heard his voice coming from the bottom of a well. "Is this for your article?"

"Why not? You swigged the lust potion to prove me wrong. I might as well take advantage of the opportunity to prove myself right."

"You're not right. I'll be fine. Give me a minute and the ephedrine rush will subside." How he managed to put that many words in correct order he'd never know, when all he could concentrate on, even with his eyes squeezed shut, was the warmth and scent coming off Zoe. She was flagrantly female, exuding a primitive allure that was more intoxicating to his senses than anything he'd ever experienced.

"Are you tingling?"

"Uh, yeah." Hell, he was vibrating.

She moved closer and his psychedelic lids flew open. "Stay away from me."

"Why?" Her smile gloated, just a touch. "Are you having trouble controlling your lust?"

He passed a hand across his eyes. "I can't look at you."

"Hmm. I need to take this down. So far we've got fever, dizziness, shortness of breath, tingling." Her gaze dropped below his belt. "And, uh, is that thing moving?"

That *thing* had a mind of its own. A one-track mind, especially when Zoe angled in for a closer look. The urge to grab hold of her and use her for unspeakable purposes blowtorched his brain.

One brittle sliver of control kept him clinging to the edge of the bench top for dear life. "Zoe, get away. I don't want you here."

"Pfft. You think I'd leave you now?"

"Go home. Please."

"But this is just getting good." She ran a hand down his rigid arm and he nearly jumped out of his skin. "It's like Dr. Jekyll and Mr. Hyde." She pressed against him. Lowered her voice. "I can see the beast coming out in you. I want to experience that, too. With you, Shane."

"You'll be sorry," he choked out.

"No, I won't."

"Then I'll be sorry," he muttered, but the lust was too much, a living, breathing force inside him that had to burst free. With a hoarse curse, Donovan let go, and passion tore through him like flames shooting out the broken windows of a burning building.

His mouth was on Zoe's before he could process the desire to kiss her. He'd always been a tentative kisser, starting slow and gentle, hoping for a gradual buildup to dancing tongues and deep plunges. But with her…

With her, he knew exactly what to do.

His tongue was in her mouth. Hers twisted alongside, warm and wet. He opened wider, opened her, too, sucking up the taste of her female essence, stingingly hot and sweet like a honeycomb. She moaned into his mouth, saying something that sounded like *the taste,* although truthfully he didn't care, couldn't stop, as the small vibration she'd made only added to the roaring, pounding rush raging inside him.

Pure lust. Like nothing he'd ever felt.

Some distant part of his brain fought against the recklessness of it all, but there was no use. He was a goner.

He spread his hands across Zoe's bottom and lifted her easily onto the bench. She was a featherweight. Right now, he believed he could have lifted an automobile single-handed.

Zoe wiggled her ass onto the countertop. Glass clinked. Donovan, always so scrupulous, couldn't make himself care. He fumbled for two seconds at the tiny buttons on her clingy little cardigan, then grew impatient and simply pushed it up, dragging the matching tank with it as she raised her arms to help. His brain short-circuited when her breasts were revealed, and he abandoned the task of undressing her to palm those naked beauties, barely taking time to flick his thumbs across the hard buds at the center before his lips closed over them, one after the other, taking quick, hard, frantic pulls.

Zoe let out a choking sound and struggled to pop her head out of the tangled garments. "Shane. Yesss. Suck them. That feels so good."

The lust was all-consuming. He fit as much of her breast into his mouth as he could, gorging himself, bending her backward across the bench surface until she was on her elbows, moaning, arching into the wet heat of his mouth with her thighs wantonly spread and her knees raised high.

She cradled the back of his head, holding him to her breast, while his hands dropped lower. A lot of the long, sheer skirt was pooled around her hips, but he was so eager he hacked through it like a jungle explorer wielding a machete, intent only on the steamy heart of her, the moist, tight opening of her sex, his only hope of relief for the thundering demands that had overtaken every cell of his being.

One sharp tug and he'd snapped the elastic of her thong. Her head jerked up and her eyes got big. "Superstrength," she sighed, and her fervent admiration told him that she was not only a more-than-willing participant but actually in awe of him.

Awe. He'd never inspired *that* before.

Incredibly his desire expanded. It wouldn't have been inconceivable for him to pound his chest and let out a roar, but that would have taken him away from his goal, and nothing was going to interfere with the rapacious demand that he sink his rock-hard cock into her tight little body.

Another of the power surges burned in his fingers, and he tore his way through the last barriers to succor— belt, trousers, shorts. His hard-on emerged at last, swollen and throbbing with need, so painfully hard it was almost purple. Zoe was owl-eyed beneath a tangle of red curls, breathing hard as she rubbed her thighs together. He pulled her knees apart and stepped between them. Took hold of her hips and slid her to the edge. She braced herself, and for one instant their eyes met and the sex became not only about lust but about Donovan and Zoe and their amazing, surprising, unconventional attraction for each other.

Even though he felt as if he'd grown ten feet, the lab

bench was still a few inches too high. He gripped her hips and slid her down, directly onto his waiting erection. For a few seconds he was too big. She squirmed against the pressure.

"Zoe," he said. Pleaded. The need to drive himself inside her was too strong. A primal fire in his veins. He fought against it, searching for the sane, cautious scientist lost in the wild man he'd become.

She clung to him with her legs wrapped around his waist. "Do it," she said, her face so close he could feel and taste her breath. Another wave of lust overtook him.

"Do it," Zoe repeated. Her eyes were filled with a fierce, blazing hunger that almost equaled his own. "Do it. Push deeper. I want all of you."

She grabbed the ledge behind her and arched into him, tightening her inner muscles and creating an inexorable suction that put an end to his moment of self-control. He pushed. She let out a low, animal-like growl, her legs and sex holding him in a vise of hot, slick flesh.

The pleasure was so intense it felt like pain. His blood, his head, throbbed with a hollow, resonating rhythm. Almost like the beat of jungle drums.

Even with the power surge that had infused his muscles, he couldn't hold Zoe up and drive as deeply into her as he wanted. He hugged her bottom, keeping her locked tight on his erection, and carried her to the desk in his office, some distant part of his barely functioning brain recognizing that privacy and staying away from case evidence were good things. With her legs opened wide and her heels caught on the edge, she lay back across his neat stacks of files in offering and he slid all the way inside her, as solidly as a closing bolt.

Her eyes were slits, the pupils pinpoints so they were all iris like a cat's. He wasn't sure she even saw him.

Until she caught his tie, wrapped it twice around the flat of her hand and yanked him to her for a needy, biting kiss. They ground against each other, hungry, panting, desperate.

The drumbeats had become a continuous roar in Donovan's head. He thrust, hearing himself shout as he came and came again, still thrusting, met every time by Zoe's clenching, spasming body.

His mind blacked out and didn't return until she moved against him. They were flat on the desktop, joined in an intimate embrace. He was still hard. And the lust remained.

She exhaled. He lowered his mouth to her breasts while he reached for the floor with his feet, thinking to disengage, but her legs tightened around him. "No, stay inside me, just like this." There was no mistaking that the words were a command, even though her voice was threaded with exhaustion.

"But, Zoe…" If he moved away, he'd have to start up again. Already the hunger was a siren call that he couldn't resist. He adjusted his position, sliding a bit deeper in the narrow passage of her wet, clinging flesh.

She gave a musical sigh. "Oh, yes. Stay."

His mouth opened on her breast. Licking, tasting, devouring. The way he felt, he could remain inside her forever.

Their desire escalated instantly. She shifted. He got

both feet firmly on the floor, nearly slipping out of her until she wiggled down, his tie still wound around her hand, and brought him home. He was lassoed, locked down, and that was exactly what he wanted.

"Do you feel it?" she asked, drawing in the tie until he was in kissing range.

Do I feel it? How could she even question that?

"It's coming back," he muttered against her neck, although the lust had never left. "Too strong."

"Not too strong."

"Very close to it." She didn't know. She couldn't possibly know because she hadn't drunk—

Although barely cognizant, his brain rebelled. The feline hormone he and Gil had discovered in the potion should have no effect. But logic and reason didn't matter to him now. Zoe was beneath him, warm, soft and fragrant, stripped naked in all the essential areas, and there was no longer room for rational, doubting thoughts in his head. The need was rising rapidly like an engulfing tide.

The palms of his hands were alive with sensation as he stroked her, sliding along her smooth body to find the center point of her pleasure. Her clit must have been raw. One touch and she jerked hard against him. He pressed lightly, rocking inside her as she climaxed with shuddering gasps.

He shut his eyes and lost himself in the rush of pure, driving lust.

"So."

Shane didn't respond. He was in the desk chair, his

head slung back, exposing the long column of his bare throat. As soon as she'd released him, he'd torn away the tie and popped a few buttons in his haste to rip open his shirt. He was still hot and sweaty. Ripe with testosterone.

Yum. Zoe ran her tongue across her lips and got another jolt of the lust potion. A warm pulse this time. The potency must be fading.

Not for Shane. He'd pulled up his pants but hadn't zipped all the way. There was a conspicuous bulge in his lap.

"So you have to agree now." She wrangled with her sweater set, lightweight cashmere-blend garments that had transformed into a harness around her shoulders and upper arms. "The potion works."

"You can't say that."

"Shane. C'mon. I was there." Finally she peeled the sweater away and separated it from the tank, which she pulled on. They hadn't even locked the doors. "It felt like a wave crashing over me and pulling me out to sea. Wicked undertow."

He squinted. "How do you know? You didn't— damn." He patted down the desk. "I lost my glasses."

"Do you need them?"

"Maybe I want to see you clearly." He frowned and rubbed his forehead. "Since I can't seem to think clearly. My brain's all foggy."

"Never mind," she soothed. "You don't have to see me. My top's back on."

His face remained grim despite her attempt to lighten

his mood. The chair creaked as he leaned back, his eyes shut again. She watched his chest rise and fall as he fought for steady breaths, each one making a hollow beneath his ribs. A delicate tracery of tingles skittered over her nerve endings, a chill, except that her skin was flushed with warmth.

After a minute a helpless moan rose from Shane. "That wasn't me."

"Then who was it? Mr. Hyde?"

"I suppose."

"Well, Mr. Hyde sure tastes a lot like you."

He pressed fingers against his eyelids. "Viagra," he muttered. "What's in it? I need to look into that, except the analysis didn't show those types of components."

Zoe smoothed wrinkles from her skirt. "You still want a logical explanation."

"There must be one. I don't do this kind of—"

Suddenly he sat forward. His face was chalk. "Dammit, Zoe, I didn't use protection. I'm sorry. I didn't even think of it, not for a second." He dropped his head onto his fists and ground his knuckles against his forehead. "Son of a bitch. I don't believe this."

Zoe's mind reeled because she hadn't thought of protection either. Never in her life had she had sex without a condom. Not once. Not even with her one long-term relationship—if six months counted as long term—because when it came down to it, she hadn't trusted that Alain, a spoiled son of a French industrialist, wouldn't cheat on her with one of the topless beauties who pranced the beaches of Cannes. Or one of Zoe's girlfriends. Or the maid. Or maybe even the innocent village girl who rented out umbrellas on the beach.

"It's all right, I think." She felt their mingled juices between her thighs. That sort of turned her on. Especially when she thought of him inside her, a seething, boiling, unstoppable force. *Mmm.*

With effort, she concentrated on the issue at hand. "I'm taking the pill."

"And I'm clean," he said. "I haven't, uh, been with that many women."

She heard the question in his voice. It was she, after all, who had the reputation. "One is all it takes," she pointed out but couldn't hold on to the presumed insult. "I've always been careful, but I've taken the test, too. My insurance requires a yearly physical."

He exhaled. "Anyway, I am sorry. I was thoughtless."

"Literally. I understand. I was the same way." Still tingling, she wrapped herself in her arms. "It was the strangest feeling. But also the best."

"It was too much. Even now…" His eyes became burning coals when he looked at her. She shivered. "You never said—how did you know about the wave?"

"Then you felt the same way?"

"More or less."

"I'm guessing more."

"Yeah."

She couldn't help looking toward his erection. She wasn't completely sated yet either. "When we kissed," she said. "It happened when we kissed. I tasted the potion in your mouth."

"Are you sure it wasn't—"

"Your overwhelming sex appeal?"

He laughed shortly. "Right."

The man had no idea. Zoe pushed her hair off her face and leaned across the desk toward him. "What do we do now?"

"You do nothing. I finish my analysis of the potion."

"How soon can you have the final results?"

"I could stay tonight and work on it, but…"

Her gaze dropped again. "You're not in any shape."

He put his hands in his lap and winced.

She offered a sultry smile. "I could help you out."

"In the lab? I can't have that."

"Gosh, no, of course not. It's okay if we screw on the desk, but don't let me near your precious test tubes." She shook her head at him, laughing all the while. "Oh, don't go worrying your pointy little head, Dr. Shane. I wasn't thinking of being your lab assistant."

She swung her legs around and slid off the desk, going down onto her knees in front of him. Her lips puckered in anticipation as she reached into his open fly. "If you don't mind."

"Lock the door," he said weakly.

Mercy, but that potion was powerful stuff. While she'd regained some of her faculties, she couldn't make herself care about being caught or losing control or even getting her story, not with Shane's stiff cock hot in her hand. Her tongue looped around the engorged head. She felt his heart pulsing, the lust throbbing, as one more time they gave in to the wild rush of the potion's demands.

Shane white-knuckled the arms of the chair. "I'm not sure I'll ever get relief." But he slumped lower onto his spine, his legs spread.

"No promises." She reached up and stroked the flat of his stomach. "But they say that the third time's the charm."

9

"WHAT TIME IS IT? I forgot about Sara and Hailey." Zoe flicked on the blinker and whipped her steering wheel around, heading for the grocery store on Thirtieth Street. "I was going to have a late dinner waiting for them."

Being thrown against his seat belt didn't stop Shane from checking his watch. "Seven twenty-seven." He paused, then added, "in the p.m.," presumably because he was as flipped out as she.

Down was up, night was day. But *in*, she thought with a giddy chuckle, was definitely not *out*. She'd had Shane in her for practically an hour straight, one way or the other, and if it wasn't for the hot dish promised to her neighbors, her only purchase would be condoms. Lots of them. That she should be making observations and taking notes for her article barely passed through her mind. This wasn't research, even if it ought to have been.

"Good," she said, touching the accelerator. She was hyped up, lighter than air, ready to rise straight out of the car, above the red-tile roofs and palms, and float over the city to the ocean. "I've got maybe half an hour. The Valentines have a long drive from Palm Springs."

Shane gripped the armrest as the car picked up speed. "I'm not going into any grocery store."

She smiled. "Why not? You're presentable." Thanks to the blow job to end all blow jobs. Not even *Balam K'am-bi* was a match for her talents in that area.

"Haven't you ever noticed how erotic a supermarket is? All those melons and cucumbers and figs."

"Figs?" Her walking around the store without underwear wouldn't do it for him?

"Someone once told me that *fig* is Italian slang for female genitalia."

"Oh, great. And here I was going to make melon-cucumber-fig salad." Laughing gaily at his expression, she gave the engine a little more gas. The wind whipped through the convertible. She *was* flying, without benefit of wings. Maybe she wouldn't have to come down to earth ever again or think about disappointing her parents and her potential.

A few minutes later she pulled into the parking lot and left Shane in the convertible, guarding his bike, which they'd stashed in her backseat, wheels spinning in the breeze. He was a different sort of guy than most she knew, conscientious about the environment in a quietly active way rather than being all talk and no follow-through like the marine biologist who wouldn't pollute his body—except with weed.

She hesitated beside the car before going in, feeling especially fond. Shane had many admirable, non-potion-enhanced qualities. "Can you see through my skirt?"

His eyes narrowed. "Do you want me to?"

She giggled. "Just tell me." It was chiffon, but there was also a modesty layer. No one should be able to tell she'd lost her unmentionables in a chemistry lab.

"I better not look." He stole a glance. "You're okay. More than okay. Pretty, with your hair all windblown like that." His voice lowered. "In fact, you're beautiful." His eyes ignited. "Very sexy."

Give him a minute and he'd be chasing her around the lot. With the skirt bunched in her hands so she wouldn't be tempted to touch him, she bent to drop a quick kiss on his forehead. His sweetly creased forehead. He was a good, earnest, thoughtful man, even with the potent traces of potion running through his veins. Maybe it was only her high talking, but she felt as if she'd fallen just a little bit in love with him.

She was a bad aim. The kiss landed on his mouth. Instantly it opened and reached up for her, his tongue darting into her mouth. A familiar heat swept over her like a desert wind. Pulling away was a supreme effort. She walked into the store with her fingertips pressed to her mouth, wondering if her feelings were real or only a result of the potion. Would they go away? *Did they have to?*

Kathryn would know. Zoe pulled out her cell phone as she arrived at the fruit-and-veg section. "Kath—I did it," she blurted when her friend answered. "I tried the lust potion."

There was a lengthy pause. Zoe heard the sounds of a restaurant in the background while Kathryn formulated her reply. "And it worked? I was afraid Jag had cheated you."

"Not that potion. We used the real one, in Shane's lab. I think we set a new record for consecutive orgasms."

"Don't be too sure of that." Zoe could hear the smile in Kathryn's voice. "But *Shane?* So you ditched the option of conducting an objective experiment with a stranger."

"I got my proof anyway." Zoe fanned her face while she looked over the array of peppers. Colorful as Christmas. Red and green and gold, all sizes. She could have strung the tiny jalapeños as a garland for her Christmas tree—if she had a tree.

"How was it?"

Zoe's gaze landed on a cucumber. "I can't go into details right now. I'm standing in the erotic section of a Vons and I'm not wearing panties."

Kathryn laughed. "I can't wait to hear the details of that one."

Zoe threw a red bell pepper into her basket. Kathryn was having a muffled conversation with a companion who sounded a lot like Coyote Sullivan. The obvious closeness between them gave her a small pang of longing. "You're at dinner? I'd better let you go. I only called to ask how long the potion lasts. Shane is still in a state, if you know what I mean."

"I know." Kathryn sounded amused. "*We* know."

"Yes, but how long?"

"For Coyote and me? One month and counting."

Zoe snorted. "Thanks. That helps a lot."

Kathryn was practically purring. "It should happen to you."

Maybe it already had. The thought was disconcerting

to Zoe as she put away the cell and added more ingredients to her basket. She'd begun the experiment for strictly professional reasons, but suddenly it seemed that she was in true danger of falling in love instead of lust.

She came down from her high with a thud. How easily she'd dismissed all thought of using the article as a springboard to respectability. Kathryn might have lightened up and fallen in love, but she'd remained a professional, invested in her career.

Zoe needed to do the same. Perhaps it was time to step back from her lust for Shane and gain an objective distance, even if the thought made her queasy. She'd have to call on the Aberdeen traits of discipline and dedication if she wanted to proceed with the original plan.

Not *if*. She did. She wanted to write that article and rise out of the rank of gossip columnist. Of course, if she didn't let herself get too distracted, there was no reason she couldn't have Shane, too. At least as long as the potion lasted….

Fifteen minutes later Zoe was in her kitchen, diverting from the recipe as she threw together a Caribbean black-bean casserole with spicy mango salsa and the accompanying fruit salad—melons, but no figs Shane was outside in the backyard waiting for Connie to sniff out his top ten favorite watering spots.

"Hey, look at us," she said when the pair of them came into her apartment. "Making dinner and walking the dog. We're almost back to normal."

Shane shoved his hands deep into his pockets. "I don't feel normal."

"You're still having symptoms?" She was back to her old self, no longer soaring on cloud nine except when he touched or kissed her. Then all bets were off. "Maybe we should call a doctor."

He flushed. "No, don't do that. As long as I keep my distance from you, I can manage."

"Oh." Did he *want* to manage?

Think about your story, not irrational, impulsive feelings. She used the white-wine vinegar as smelling salts. "What about other women? Does any random female do it for you or is the potion selective with its urges?"

"How would I know?" The question had befuddled Shane. "I don't want just any random female."

A pleasure warmed her from the inside out. Not the lust potion's brand of heat—a different kind of warmth. "Thank you. That's kind of a romantic thing to say, considering."

He didn't get that she was serious. "Considering that a little over an hour ago I was tearing your clothes off?" He glanced at her, then quickly away, making a face at himself. "My behavior was—was—"

Thrilling, she thought, but said, "Don't apologize. You couldn't help it." *Make a note. In large doses,* Balam K'am-bi *is hell on the lingerie budget.*

"I'd better go, before we...you know. Get overwhelmed."

"Maybe that's a good idea." She didn't want him to go, but she did need to keep a clear head. "We don't want to be inappropriate in front of the dog."

"Okay. Sure." He turned one way, then the other,

looking as if he wanted to say something but was at a loss for words because he was a logical man and there was no logical explanation for what was happening. "I'll, uh, go—"

She pointed with a leafy bunch of cilantro. "The door's that way."

He looked miserable. "See you later?"

"Yes, later." But maybe sooner than he expected. She could only be sensible for so long.

DONOVAN STARED AT THE FOUR walls of his living room from the depths of a Danish chair that angled so close to the floor his knees were higher than his ears. He'd taken a shower, alternating between steamy hot and icy cold to shock his body into submission. Drying off had resulted in jerking off, and even that had helped for only a short while. Next, he'd forced down two chicken salad sandwiches, hoping the bread would soak up the remains of the potion that still seemed to bubble in his gut. Yet every time he thought of Zoe, his temperature spiked, his blood pounded, his cock swelled and—bingo—he was right back where he'd started.

A conclusion was hammering at his skull, demanding acknowledgement: *The potion is real.*

But he wouldn't let the idea in. He absolutely refused. Despite the animal pheromones that had been added to the second sample he'd tested, there was no reasonable scientific explanation for such a possibility.

Then how did he explain the sudden and inexplicable flirtation between Gil and Mandy Rae, who'd never given the boy the time of day?

And how to explain his own state of arousal? Simple, ordinary lust? He had dreamed of making love to Zoe for a long time. Having her in reality had blown his mind. Maybe he was only experiencing an outpouring of too much dammed-up testosterone. The "potion" had tapped into desires that already existed and provided a convenient, permissable sexual outlet.

Yes, that made sense.

He looked down into his lap and sighed. With a boner like this and a woman like that, he could only be sensible for so long.

"WHAT'S NEW AROUND HERE?" Sara Valentine asked after they'd finished talking about her father's operation and her mother's penchant for turning every visit into a soap-opera drama starring herself. Sara was almost fifty, generous of nature, humor and figure. She was the office manager for a team of corporate lawyers, ten years divorced, a Telemundo devotee and exasperated mother of an almost-eighteen-year-old who'd been going through an awkward phase for the past six years.

"Not much." Zoe dished up the fruit salad for Hailey, who'd grumpily refused the black-bean casserole. Too much junk food during their car trip, according to her mother, even though Hailey swore she was still on a diet.

Sara ladled on the salsa and dug into the casserole with gusto. Any meal she didn't have to cook was good enough for her. "There were no more run-ins with Donovan?"

"The opposite, actually. He was a help with Connie."

"There's a surprise. Don't tell me you two have finally made friends."

Zoe was dying to say that they'd made more than that. She wasn't much good at keeping secrets. But Hailey was listening, even while plugged into an iPod. The young woman had expressed a great interest in everything about Zoe. After many a fight with her mom, she'd visited upstairs to gripe about the unfairness of it all and how she wished she could live like Zoe.

"Sort of," Zoe said. She caught her bottom lip with her teeth, then let go. It was still tender.

Sara narrowed her eyes beneath a thick crop of curls caught up in a barrette. "Something's different about you. Did you get collagen injected in your lips?"

A fat strawberry dropped off Hailey's spoon into her dish. Only a week ago they'd had a discussion about how many of her high school classmates were going in for plastic surgery. Zoe had come down on the side of learning to love your flaws. Hailey, with a broad nose and a pudge, had said that was easy when you didn't have any. Zoe had skimmed back her hair from her face to exhibit her too-long nose and pointy chin. Camouflaged, she claimed, by her sparkling personality.

"Absolutely not." Zoe shook her head vehemently. "I'd never."

"I don't know," Sara said. "You have that bee-stung look. As if—" She stopped, blinked, then clapped her mouth shut around a forkful of rice, beans and chorizo.

Hailey peeled off her earpieces. "As if what?"

"I ate too many peppers," Zoe said.

Hailey wasn't convinced. "No one ever tells me anything. I'll be eighteen in three weeks. I'm old enough."

Sara stepped in, quick with the distraction from long experience. "Thanks for dinner, Zoe, honey. And taking care of the dog."

"My pleasure."

"You said Donovan helped?" Sara's smile was knowing.

"Uh-huh."

"Mr. Shane, the bike dude from upstairs?" Hailey asked. "My friends think he's a forty-year-old virgin."

Zoe sucked in her cheeks until they were hollow, then released them with a *smack*. "Unh. He's in his early thirties, I'm pretty sure."

"I thought he was older, too," Sara said. "No wonder he wasn't interested in going out with Birgitta."

Birgitta was Sara's best friend, a six-foot Swedish Pilates instructor with shoulders like a linebacker. She had at least ten years on Shane.

"Birgitta's definitely not his type," Zoe said.

"But we know who is, don't we, Hailey?"

The girl shrugged. "Zoe can do better. She knows famous people."

"Famous people are short." Zoe fished a slice of kiwi from the dish. "And usually not half as interesting as their publicity."

Sara cackled. "Is there something wrong with short?" She was round, brown and squat, like a lawn troll without the pointy hat. She'd bought one to put on the doorstep as a joke. Hailey had "accidentally" smashed it to pieces. Her mother mortified her. Zoe had sympathized, since *her* mother used to speak Tlingit and Bantu in public. And frame her daughter's report cards. And wear *kinta* cloth instead of Burberry plaid like the other mothers.

Zoe touched her fingers to her tear ducts. "You can't be short. Your personality is too big." She blinked. "Have you ever noticed how your perception of a person's looks changes as you get to know their character? Beautiful people can become ugly or at least bland. And…"

"Nerds become hunks?" Sara suggested.

Hailey wrinkled her nose. "Ewww."

"Maybe," Zoe said. A goofy smile took over her face. She blushed the way schoolgirls used to blush before jock posses and rainbow parties came into vogue. Although she'd have liked to blame her warm cheeks on the potion's heat, she knew she couldn't. Despite her resolutions to get serious about the article, all she really wanted was to get serious with Shane.

AFTER DINNER WAS OVER Hailey stepped into the building's foyer with Zoe. She had Falcon on a leash, but he was too excited by his owner's return to behave. They had to hop and high-step to get out of entanglements as he wound in and out of their feet.

"You're going back to school tomorrow?" Zoe asked, lifting a foot. She'd only had to glance up the tile-paved stairway to Shane's apartment and her palms had become damp and tingly. The potion wasn't out of her system yet.

"I thought I might as well miss the entire week, but Mom said no. She wants me to get my stupid homework and be a wallflower all weekend." The dog tugged Hailey toward the front door, which was oak with a Spanish Mission arch and a small window caged by an iron grille. "It's not like I was off having fun at Grandma's house."

Zoe gave the girl a sympathetic smile. "Welcome to the world of family responsibilities."

"I wish I was like you—living on my own, with a cool job and a wicked car."

"Independence is fun. But being alone isn't." Zoe stepped over the straining leash, struck by the truth in her statement. She'd been lonely for male companionship and hadn't completely realized it until she'd hooked up with Shane and discovered how entertaining even a solid, serious scientist could be. "Hold out a while longer. You'll be in college soon."

"Yeah, but Mom says I should live at home to save money." Hailey pulled the door open. "Can you maybe talk to her? I'll be totally out of it if I don't live in the dorms."

"We'll see." Zoe started up the steps. "Catch you tomorrow. Don't go too far with Connie." Their eclectic North Park neighborhood was decent but hardly upscale, safe during daylight hours, though the nights could be dicey in some areas, especially when your guard dog was twenty pounds of fur and attitude.

Instead of going home, Zoe wiped her hands on her skirt and knocked on Shane's door. He answered with wet hair and a pinched expression, wearing the same terry-cloth robe over baggy shorts.

Cold shower, she decided. "I thought I'd better check on you. How are you feeling?"

He made a sheepish face. "Like an idiot. I'm going to lose my job if anyone finds out what I did."

"Why should they? You said you freeze-dried the samples and what was in the beaker was leftover. So it's not like you drank *all* of the evidence and have to confess in open court."

That only made him groan. "Don't you see how bad this is?"

"Hmm. I thought it was pretty good." She grabbed both ends of his dangling tie belt and tugged him closer. "Spectacular, even."

"It was. We were. But what I did to make *us* happen was a colossal mistake."

"Oh." She licked the roof of her mouth. "I suppose we could stop now and go on as if none of it happened. If that's what you want."

"That's not what I want."

She looked down at the tent in his shorts. "So I see."

"What was that you said about teaching me how to break the rules?"

"How to misbehave." Slowly she wound the fabric belt around her hands and wrists until they were bound together, nose to nose, breast to chest, erection to belly. The miracle of physiology—their parts functioned best when in a pair. "But you can't misbehave without breaking a few rules." She breathed against his mouth. "Can you?"

For a moment his face showed the struggle of the

conscientious scientist, but the potion was still too strong in him.

He said, "I'm sold," and kissed her, diving into it like an Olympian, with lots of twisting tongue and a plunge into a whirling arousal that rose up fast around them, closing over their heads, shutting out the questions.

She wound her arms around his waist. He swept her inside, actually lifting her off her feet for a heady moment, then slammed the door by collapsing back against it, still kissing her and kissing her, his hands cupping and kneading her derriere.

"Your obligations," he gasped. "You're finished?"

"The Valentines? Yeah. I delivered."

"Good. Because I'm not letting you out of here until morning."

She let out a hoot of exhilaration as he picked her up and sort of slung her over his shoulder, a position that only got them more entangled, with her hands bound and his robe bunching open. They crossed to the bedroom—at least she assumed they must have, because she wasn't paying attention to anything but the authority in his grip and the thrilling ripple of muscle beneath her hands.

He bounced her down on the bed, letting the robe slide off over his head. His chest wasn't massive, nor hairy like some of the man-beasts she'd dated over the years. Shane was like a greyhound—smooth, lean and taut with muscle where it counted. She'd never date a gorilla again.

He hovered above her. There was a ripping sound and

then he flung away the robe. The belt was still wrapped around her wrists and hands, and he used that to his advantage, pulling her arms over her head and tying her to the turned-wood rails of the headboard.

Her eyes became round. "Shane."

He gave her a tight, smug smile. "I said all night and I meant all night."

She wiggled her wrists. "You don't think I'd run, do you?"

"I'm not taking the chance." His mouth opened over hers and he speared her with his tongue. She wanted to catch hold and suck. He pulled away. "But I'll make you glad to be stuck here with me."

"That's easy. I already am." She arched her torso off the bed, stretching her arms to the limit of the restraints. Trying to reach him or at least lure him into touching her again. She wanted his hands, his mouth, his cock. All of him and all at once.

That wasn't Shane's plan. He retreated out of range. "First, the skirt. Pretty and all, but I like it better when you show your legs."

The boho-chic garment, picked up cheaply at Kobey's Swap Meet, had an elastic waistband. Easy removal. He pulled the skirt past her hips, down her legs. She kicked free of the fabric. He stared in consternation at the nude bikini panties she'd slipped on somewhere in between chopping peppers and slicing melons—as if he'd expected less. Or more, depending what he'd wanted to see.

Zoe giggled. This was all so confusing.

She pressed her thighs together. There was a darkly savage look in Shane's eyes. He flexed his hands.

"Don't rip them," she said. "I can't afford to go through underwear at this rate."

"I'll buy you new ones." He took hold of the panties on either side and tore them open, jerking her hips off the bed to do so.

Her heart went thump. Making a rough purring sound in his throat, he scraped away the shreds of material and stretched-out curls of elastic, leaving her naked from the waist down except for one dangling sandal.

She flicked the shoe away. What the hell. If she was going to be brazen, she was going to do it right.

"Okay," she said. "You've got me where you want me, Mr. Hyde. What are you going to do now?"

Her arms were already pulled about a foot apart. She opened her legs wider. All the way, so her insteps balanced at the very edges of the mattress. She hummed, saying softly, almost as if to herself, "Uh-huh, what *are* you going to do?"

Shane had been kneeling at the foot of the bed. When she spread-eagled herself, he came forward, stretching on all fours. He looked at her for a moment, then closed his eyes and inhaled. His body quivered with tension.

Zoe held herself still. Her lungs hurt as if a steel band had been drawn around her chest. She was warm everywhere else—warm like a tropical rain, melting and dripping with the need to have Shane take her hard and fast.

He pounced. The rosy head of his penis was pearled by arousal and poking out the slit in his boxer shorts. As he rolled on top of her, licking and sucking and squeezing, she was transfixed by the slick trail he left across her bare stomach.

"I want you inside me." She spasmed, pulling against the knots. Although normally Shane was the kind of guy who'd leave her wiggle room, he'd tied her securely. He was serious about not letting her get away. She wasn't sure if she liked that or not, but there was no denying that being *truly* at his mercy made the edge of their uncontrollable desire a little bit sharper.

"I want you—"

He smothered her mouth with his own. She could do nothing but allow it—this long stream of kisses that he showered over her face until she was floating in an endless sea of pleasure. She'd slipped out of her head, had missed him stripping and donning a condom, but suddenly he was there, poised between her thighs, asking her without words if she wanted him, and her body sang the answer, strung taut and open and wet as he entered her with a slow, gliding thrust.

"Aah." Her hands clenched, then sprang open.

"I always wanted this to happen," he said with his face tucked between her cheek and her shoulder. "Right here, in my bed." He pushed just a little deeper, then slid his hands out from under her and braced himself. "Hold on. We're going for a wild ride."

The band of cloth tightened as she pulled against it,

twisting her wrists to lock her fingers around the knobs in the rails. "The lust potion? *Still?*"

He winced, rocking experimentally to set an intoxicating rhythm. "It hasn't gone away."

He believed.

He *had* to.

But only while in the throes. It was easy to then.

And easy to moan like a wild creature and writhe and bite, if only at air. Zoe was a woman of many adventures and yet she was shocked at herself this go-round. If she hadn't been tied down, she'd have been on him like a wildcat, and that couldn't be only the potion because she'd had a much smaller dose. The beast in him had brought out the beast in her.

The lust was a rampaging fever. It seemed incredible that anyone survived.

They were mating with such ferocity now that the headboard banged against the wall. The reverberations traveled from Zoe's fists to her spine and into her womb. The first small spasmic quivers became a full-fledged climax that streaked through her like a lightning storm, and still she wanted something more.

Shane's body, all smooth, hard muscle, had risen above hers as his arms stiffened and he threw back his head to howl. She lifted her hips to him, doing the best she could, when suddenly what she wanted was to hold his face and make him see her, really see *her,* not the party girl or the potion partner or the irritating neighbor who'd nevertheless gotten under his skin.

But he was too far gone. He was pumping, filling her

with a heat that blossomed outward from her center in rapidly unfolding layers. Her clit burned for his touch. She dug in her heels. Bit back a cry as he withdrew.

He stopped, hovering above her. "Again?"

She curled her tongue against her top lip. "Never stop."

Incredibly he'd remained hard. He reentered her in one smooth push. She moaned with gratefulness, feeling as if she could come a hundred times between now and morning.

"Untie me."

"Why?"

"I have to touch you."

"We're touching where it counts."

"Not really."

He gave her a look. Pleasant surprise. But all he said was, "Quit pulling," as he worked at the knots.

She squeezed down on his cock. He pulled her wrists free but held on to them, kissing the red marks until she clasped his face in her hands. "Lift me up," she said softly, and he caught her around the waist and tipped them both into a sitting position. They were entwined. Intimately and irrevocably entwined.

Zoe stared into Shane's eyes. Had she ever done this? Looked directly at a man while he was deep inside her? Always, it seemed, she'd had her eyes closed. But with Shane she wanted the full intimacy.

She felt his pounding heart. His ragged breathing. His throbbing cock.

His hands spread across her buttocks. "This isn't the potion."

It was, but it was also so much more. She couldn't put her emotion into words, could only shake her head. And kiss him, completing their coupling with a slow grinding motion that set off the second wave of a release that quaked and rippled and spread, swallowing them up in ecstasy.

10

"COFFEE," ZOE CROAKED FROM the bed in a voice like a toad. "I need coffee."

"That could be a problem," Donovan said, already up and showered. He'd been standing beside the bed, watching her sleep, actually envying the pillow hugged to her naked breasts. "There's probably only instant in the cupboard. I don't drink the stuff often."

"You don't?" She flailed among the sheets. "That does it. We're over. I can handle a man who prefers bicycles to convertibles, even spinach to sugar, but no caffeine? Impossible." She peeped out at him. "Do you have Diet Coke?"

"Nope."

"Horrors. You're one of those health-nut types, aren't you? I've noticed the signs."

"I may be."

She groaned. "Things are looking different in the bright light of a decaffeinated morning."

Even though he knew she was being dramatic, the words struck too close to home. In the shower, he'd started questioning himself again. What if it was only the lust potion? What if Zoe woke up with regrets?

So he was noncommittal and said, "They frequently do," while he went to the closet and unhooked a fresh pair of khakis.

Zoe watched him step into them. "You seem limber enough. I'm a puddle of twanging goo." She mewed pitifully. "And weak as a kitten without my jolt of caffeine."

"I'll run out and get you a latte and a croissant."

"No, no. Never let it be said that I can't make do." She climbed out of bed, shedding the sheet without a shred of inhibition. Her body was rosy and soft, slightly fuller in the breasts and bottom than he remembered, perhaps because they'd gorged themselves on sex. He was a bit swollen and tender himself.

"There's coffee at my place," she continued. "One of the benefits of boffing the neighbor is being able to run home for provisions." She lifted her hair off her neck and twisted this way and that, studying herself in the mirror over his dresser. Pink love bites dotted her body. "Huh. Looks like someone got kind of overenthusiastic."

"I have an excuse."

"The lust potion?"

"Nope." He came up from behind and squeezed her luscious heart-shaped ass. "You're too sexy for your skin."

She chuckled and spun away from him, dancing and singing, "I'm too sexy for my skin," all the way into the adjoining bathroom.

Donovan sat on the bed. How'd he get so lucky? Even losing his job might be worth it. The memory of the past twenty-four hours would keep him warm for the next fifty years.

"Will you go over to my place and put on a pot of coffee?" Zoe called over the sound of the drumming shower.

"Sure. Where's the key?"

"Hmm. I guess I didn't lock up last night when I went down to the Valentines'."

He went to the doorway. Zoe was a slender shadow behind the shower curtain. "That's not good."

"I had other things on my mind." She poked out a head, frothy with shampoo. "Shouldn't be a problem as long as Hailey remembered to lock the downstairs door."

"I'll go see."

She flashed a wet leg. "You're not even tempted? Does that mean we finally ran the potion dry?"

"I was trying to be considerate, seeing as you're a puddle of decaffeinated goo."

"Yeah, yeah." She twitched the curtain back into place. "Go make me coffee and we'll see if I have energy for a quickie."

Donovan walked over to Zoe's apartment. The door was unlocked. The place was a colorful jumble of floor pillows, lawn chairs, a grandma sofa and junk-shop furnishings painted in shades of chartreuse, pink and turquoise. On the equally colorful walls, dramatic African art hung side by side with paint-by-number kitsch and vintage drag-racing posters.

It was a mess to Donovan, but after a moment he realized that there was nothing obviously out of place. Even the stack of hardcover picture books that made a side table were arranged in ascending size. The mismatched colors and furnishings gave an image of chaos, while closer inspection revealed touches of order and culture among the wackiness. Zoe's bag had been dumped on a cheap chaise longue made of webbing and aluminum, a match to the one she kept in the backyard for her erotic nature-girl sunbathing sessions.

He went to the kitchen. The walls were yellow and the cabinets blue. She had almost nothing in them, save neat rows of spice bottles. Anise, cayenne, cumin, dill, right down the alphabet. He checked the fridge. A gigantic jar of dill pickles swimming in murk, a wedge of cheese, milk past its expiration date. The freezer. Coffee beans, Push Pops and vodka. Even the ice trays were empty.

"Did you find the coffee?" she called from the living room.

He glanced, then looked again. She wore one of his towels tucked under her armpits, showing a good inch of butt cheek. "You crossed the hallway like that?" he heard himself ask in a scolding manner even though he could've sworn that after last night he'd never be uptight again.

"I checked for tenants first, but, darn, there weren't any." She winked, playing the inveterate tease. He was beginning to realize that many of her flippant remarks sprang from an attempt to keep those around her off-kilter so they wouldn't delve into the inner workings of what made her tick. But he wanted to know. She couldn't hold him off forever.

For the time being, he shook the bag of gourmet beans and asked lightly, "Were you a nudist in another life?"

"I'm a nudist in this life. When you used to traipse the Riviera and party in Rio during Carnivale, showing a little skin is no big deal."

So her party habits had once been international. He wasn't particularly surprised, but that didn't bode well for any kind of shared future. Opposites might attract, but they rarely melded very well over the long haul.

"What were you doing in those places?" he asked, although he meant *who*. He would have blamed the potion for bringing out the macho, possessive male in him, except that he'd long nurtured a strong dislike for Zoe's boyfriends.

"Spending my trust fund," she said airily. "Avoiding reality."

He dumped beans into the grinder that sat on the countertop. "Is *this* reality?" He stood in the kitchen doorway, indicating her circus of an apartment. "Looks surreal to me."

"Are you really that narrow-minded?" She bent over, loosened her turban towel and vigorously dried her hair.

"You're right. I'm being a prude. Your lifestyle is your own." He turned to switch off the machine. "And surely not mine."

"Yeah, but you're the one who wanted some excitement in his," she called from the bathroom.

He rinsed out the carafe, filled the well, used a paper towel as a filter since there were none and measured out a scoop of coffee grounds. In between bouts of sex she'd said something vague about her reasons for writing about the lust potion, something about being taken seriously. That was the Zoe he needed to question. Perhaps he was being too hasty and they weren't the opposites he'd always assumed.

He followed her into the bathroom. "Yeah, but you—"

He stopped. She was staring at the open medicine cabinet. "Were you going through my stuff? Maybe checking out my medical history?" She shot him a puckered grin. "I'll have you know, every woman gets cystitis at least once."

"I didn't come in here," he said.

"No? Then someone else did."

"How can you tell?"

"Because I have this quirk. Okay, it's a compulsion. My inner Aberdeen neat freak, clawing to get out." She pointed. "I always put my pill bottles in alphabetical order. And now they're not."

"So you made a mistake."

"Maybe." She looked around the bathroom, frowned, then went to the bedroom.

Donovan followed. He'd always wanted to see Zoe's bedroom.

It was the opposite of his. Fucshia walls, zebra rug, a neatly made bed, turned down to show the polka-dot sheets. Clothing exploded from a half-open closet door.

She whipped off the towel and opened a drawer. "Oh," he said, startled. She turned to look at him with a lace bra in hand. "I didn't mean to follow you to watch you dress. I thought—"

"It's okay. You can watch me dress if you want."

"I thought you were looking for signs of a break-in. Like that overturned waste can."

"Connie did that. I forgot to pick it up." She stepped into a thong. "What makes you believe there was a break-in?"

"Never mind." Donovan backed out. Sheesh. He always forgot that women thought in zigzags, never following the straight, logical path.

He went to get the coffee. He was pouring it into a *Make Love, Not War* mug when she appeared, dressed in a button-down shirt she'd knotted instead of buttoning and a patterned cotton skirt that skimped on fabric. She carried pink Keds and a pair of high-heeled sandals. "Which do you think?"

"What are you doing today?"

"Desk work. Writing a column, working the phones. I have a call in to a professor of anthropology who might be able to help me hunt down the elusive history of *Balam K'am-bi*. So I should wear the tennies."

"How did you come to that conclusion?" He was baffled anew.

"Because there won't be anyone to admire how my legs look in high heels," she said. "Isn't that obvious?" She shook her head. "Men."

She went into the living room to grab her bag. "I'll take both pairs. For flexibility."

He brought her the coffee. "I hope you drink it black."

"With lots of sugar." She rummaged through her gear.

"Your wallet's there?"

"Sure." She pulled it out.

"Money's there?"

"You're still thinking there was a break-in because my pill bottles were mixed up? That's cockeyed. What thief comes in and rearranges the medicine cabinet?" While she was talking, she splayed the wallet for him, displaying a meager stash of cash.

He took the wallet, attracted to the photos in a plastic sleeve. "Your family?"

"That's them."

A freckled, baby-faced Zoe in a school uniform and horn-rimmed glasses sat on a couch with a red-haired woman who looked like a mature, somewhat thickened version of Zoe, if she took to wearing long skirts and sensible shoes in her dotage. The woman's smile was broad, and she squinted behind her glasses. Standing behind them was a young man—a redheaded popinjay in a crested blazer—and a father in tweeds, who posed in profile like Winston Churchill with a pipe and a waistcoat.

"They look like nice people." Not at all what he'd expected. Very East Coast intellectual. There was even a wall of books.

"They were." She bent to put on the Keds.

"Were?" he asked before he remembered that she'd hinted at that before, very briefly.

"They're gone. Car accident on the turnpike." Her voice was muffled. "I was twenty and about to get my master's."

"I'm sorry. That must have been hell for you."

She was clear-eyed when she straightened, but she passed the back of her wrist under her nose. "Well, you know. Either you deal with it or you go to Rio. I went to Rio."

Donovan didn't know what to say, even though he was on the verge of learning more about the inner Zoe. He'd never been much good in social situations that called for comforting platitudes. Or, let's face it, getting people to open up, since he was too buttoned-down himself.

She took back the wallet and added it to a small stash in her lap. "Everything's accounted for. Even my keys." After sniffing a tissue, she tossed it away. "The fake lust potion. The inside of my purse reeks of…huh. That's odd." Puzzlement crossed her face.

"What is it?"

She looked up, her eyes pulled into a narrow squint that was just like her mother's. "The lust potion is missing."

"YOU DON'T HAVE TO COME, Shane. I'm wearing the tennies. I can make a fast getaway if I need to."

"I'm coming." He was stalwart.

"If Jag's there, you'll only scare him away."

"Me? Scary?"

Zoe cast an amused smirk. "I'm learning that you can be *mucho* macho when you want to be." She watched Jag's storefront through the midday crowds. Her toes tapped nervously. "Trust me on this. He was wary about selling the potion to me last time I went. If a guy's with me, he'll never talk."

"I can be your ardent lover."

"You certainly can."

They exchanged smiles. Shane squeezed her hand. "Let me do this with you."

After she'd discovered that the bottle of counterfeit

potion had gone missing, they'd debated the possible scenarios, including who would want the potion and why. When she'd broached the option of returning to Jag's to find out what she could, Shane had insisted on calling in late to work to accompany her. Particularly after she'd explained how paying for the fake potion with a check had given the man her address. Why Jag would want the counterfeit potion back was a puzzle, until they'd realized that he might have been hoping to find the bottle that had been turned over to the police.

So now Shane was being all manly and protective. She liked it.

"All right. We'll try it. But don't act too smart." She lowered her sunglasses. "Take off your glasses and mess up your hair. That'll give you an unfocused, blissed-out look."

"But the potion was fake. I wouldn't be blissed-out. I'd be pissed. We might get more of a reaction if we press the matter and threaten to call the cops."

"Only as a last resort." She stepped off the curb, following the pedestrians at the crosswalk. "Try it my way first."

They sauntered into the shop. A couple of tourists browsed the merchandise. Zoe went straight to the cash register, attended by a woman who might be Jag's mother, sister or wife. She had the same timeless wrinkled brown skin and watchful eyes. A flowered scarf was tied around the shoulders of a gaudy silk blouse in a clashing pattern. She was busy with a stack of boxes and a labeling gun, her bony elbows sticking out like chicken wings.

"Hi," Zoe said. She lifted the shades. "I'm a frequent customer." Her voice lowered. "A *special* customer. Is Jag around?"

The woman barely looked up. "No Jaguar."

"But I have an urgent need to speak to Jag." Zoe smiled hopefully.

"There is no Jag here." The woman's accent was South American, but Zoe couldn't distinguish beyond that.

Shane pressed closer. "We need a refund." Zoe tapped her heel against his shin. "Or at least a replacement."

"No refunds. No exchanges."

"Forget the refund. I just want to talk to Jag about—" Zoe cleared her throat and dropped her voice to a husky whisper *"—Balam K'am-bi."*

The woman pulled the trigger on the pricing gun, giving no sign of recognition.

"I'll pay big bucks."

Zoe's offer was met with a head shake. "There's no such thing."

"That's for sure," Shane said in a loud voice. "The stuff's a total rip-off."

"Now, honey," Zoe said.

"How much did you pay already? And it didn't even work." He waved toward the door. "I oughta get one of the cops in here. I hear there's been trouble over this fake potion before. They might be interested in how you're bilking your customers."

The woman didn't seem perturbed by the threat except for a darting glance toward the back of the shop. "No refund. No potion. You go away now."

"I'm sorry," Zoe said. "He's just agitated because, well, we got sort of hooked on the potion, y'know? We didn't come to—to cause trouble." She faltered. The curtain to the back room had twitched open a half inch, revealing a sliver of oiled bald head and raisin eye. "We'd just really like another bottle of the good stuff. Genuine *Balam K'am-bi.* Please?"

Suddenly the woman released a torrent of Spanish-sounding invective. She waved her arms, shooing them toward the door. Zoe and Shane stepped out of flailing distance, but they wouldn't go.

A man charged out of the back room. He was about Zoe's height, five-six, but built like a bowling ball on tree stumps. He wore camo pants and combat boots. A shiny black T-shirt threatened to burst at the seams. "Jag's not here," he said with a voice that rumbled like a Mack truck. "Time for you to leave."

"Vaya," said the woman. *"Vaya!"*

The bowling ball brushed past them—Zoe would have gladly leaped into a gutter to get out of his way—and threw open the door. "You have to go. You're upsetting Tia."

Zoe stuck out her chin. She would have gotten up in the bouncer's face, but Shane caught her around the elbow. "How can I reach Jag? We have urgent business."

The man's black eyes were as shiny as the heavy gold chain draped around his thick neck. He had close-cropped black hair and dusky skin. His snarl revealed a row of small square teeth like abacus beads, both black and white. "Forget it. For your own good, forget you were ever here. Jag's out of that business for good."

Shane shouldered past Zoe. "And who are you?"

The man's jaw bulged. The beads clicked. "Your worst nightmare," he said, gleefully menacing.

Probably thrilled that he'd gotten to use a line from his favorite movie, Zoe thought as he escorted them out with the sweep of one meaty paw.

On the sidewalk, Zoe and Shane exchanged a look, mutually agreeing to keep quiet as they hotfooted it back to the car, slotted in a parking lot a street away.

"Did I overplay it?" he asked once they were settled in the convertible.

"You did good, actually. You drew Jag out. I saw him peeking out from the other side of the curtain. At least I think it was him."

"You should have told me. I could've nabbed him."

"How would you have gotten past the bouncer?"

"Easy. Cut him down with my superior intellect."

She chuckled. "Next time I'd like to see that in action. But never mind about nabbing Jag. *That* would have been overplaying it. We don't even know for sure that he's involved."

"Putting aside the fact that a tourist trap shouldn't need a bouncer, we are certain that someone swiped the fake potion out of your purse. That didn't happen at my lab. Did anyone approach you in the grocery store?"

"Only the vegetable guy. He wanted to talk figs."

"Zoe…"

"All right! I'll be serious." She started the car. "I'll

drop you at work. On the way, we can go over the options for our next move."

"Options? Are there any?"

"Of course. Something's fishy, right? We know the potion's the key, and therefore Jag. We just have to figure out what part he plays in all this."

"I think you're making assumptions."

She put on her sunglasses as she drove out onto the sunny street. "Here's the chronology. First, Jag drops the genuine potion in my bag, conveniently removing the evidence from under the cops' noses when they dropped by to question him about that very thing. The potion goes to the police, via my pal Ethan and on to you."

"I know all this."

"Wait. Follow along. Next, I return to Jag's and buy more potion, which turns out to be fake. But as far as he knows I still have the real potion, right?" She snapped her fingers. "Because he recognized me when I went back to buy more of the potion. He said, 'It was you.'"

"You're saying that Jag wants it back."

"Could be. He has my address from the check I wrote, so he might have gone to my apartment to steal it himself. Even though we didn't see any signs of tampering at the front door or the windows."

"But you went back to buy more, so presumably the first potion is gone. Plus, he's been selling the 'real' potion to a select clientele all along, so why would he care that you used up the bottle he dropped in your purse? In fact, it would be to his advantage if you did." Shane motioned. "*Poof.* The evidence disappears."

Zoe deflated. "Good point. But that leaves us nowhere." She ran the sequence through her mind, certain she was missing something.

"If the thief realized the potion in your purse was a fake, that would at least explain why he also searched your medicine chest."

"Oh, wow. I just remembered. Jag was demanding cash, but suddenly he was willing to take a check. Right after I mentioned that I *hadn't* used all of the potion yet. So he for sure believes that I still have it."

"Aha. Now we're getting somewhere."

She tapped her nails on the steering wheel. "But why would he want the potion back in the first place?"

"Simple. He's worried you'll turn it over to the police. He knows the sample they took of the counterfeit might get him arrested for fraud, but not possession of illegal substances. Maybe your sample can."

"Of course," Zoe said. She looked over at Shane with an I-told-you-so grin. "And I'm glad to see that you're coming around about to the possibility that there is a real lust potion."

His tie flipped in the breeze. "I'm reserving judgment for the time being."

"Yeah? Well, certain parts of you seem quite convinced to me."

"Certain parts of me don't think rationally."

She reached over and squeezed his thigh. "Thank goodness for that."

ZOE PROMISED SHANE SHE wouldn't return to Jag's without him, or do anything else to put herself in jeopardy. Which was probably just as well, since otherwise she might have followed any crazy impulse that came to mind. Instead she wrote her weekend column, e-mailed it to the copy desk and spent a couple of hours surfing the Internet for clues to the origin of *Balam K'ambi* since she still hadn't been able to get in touch with the anthropology professor. Other than finding fascinating tidbits on Mayan people and culture, the search was fruitless. The lust potion appeared to be a well-kept secret.

She moved on to researching Jag and was able to track down city records that said his shop was leased to a company called Acat Inc. By then, it was time to leave work, so she saved the information to a file and shut down her computer. Luckily Barbara Bitterman had been out of the office most of the day so she hadn't been around to press Zoe for results.

Which was what she ought to be doing to Shane. Zoe swiveled away from the desk, checking once more for lurking editrixes while she pulled the strap of her bag over her head. She was eager to get home, not only to shower hugs and kisses on Shane but to tell him about her day's work and share her growing excitement that the story was developing into something big.

That was new to her—having a rapport, sharing good conversations instead of only good times. But she had to keep in mind that they were operating under the influence of the lust potion. How real was any of this?

Not a question she was ready to face.

She ran into Ethan Ramsey outside the *Times* building, buying a tissue-paper cone of flowers from a street vendor. She approached him from behind, put her chin on his shoulder and asked, "For the girlfriend?"

Ethan grinned. "A gentleman always brings flowers."

"Especially if he's been a bad boy."

His brows went up in a *Who, me?* expression. "I'm an angel."

"You're a devil in angel's clothing." She looped an arm through his as they walked toward the fountains at Horton Plaza. "How's it going between you and Nicole? Lusty as ever?"

"Lusty?"

"I know you two used the potion."

Ethan rubbed his jaw. "Not intentionally. Some of it was spilled and I happened to be at hand." His blue eyes twinkled. "Lucky timing for me."

"Uh-huh. So it was only that once, but you're still seeing her?"

"Am I being interviewed? Kathryn told me you're writing an article about the potion."

"I could use an interview, but this isn't it. I'm asking more for personal reasons. I'm, um, trying to figure out how long the potion lasts. Kathryn and Coyote still seem to be under the influence, but they had more of the potion to work with."

Ethan slowed. "It's difficult to explain. I can't say I'm quite as out of my head as I was at first—" He broke off to flash a wicked, dimpled grin. "One of these days, remind me to tell you about how I wound up on Nicole's balcony, drooling on the window glass." They stopped and looked up at the tall Christmas tree decked out for the holidays. "Can we talk later? It's been a long day. I'm off to meet Nicole at Sky Room in La Jolla."

"Ooh—ritzy. All right." Zoe patted his cheek. He was more disheveled than usual, but she could see that the thought of Nicole put spring into his step. "You've been working too hard. Or maybe playing too hard. I've hardly seen you lately."

"There's been a rash of poisonings in the city and surrounding areas," Ethan said. "Not fatal until the past week, when a body turned up. Big story."

Zoe had been following the coverage. She'd even mentioned the case to Shane, but he'd been close-mouthed, saying only that the poison victim's blood work-up hadn't come through his lab. She could tell he'd been disappointed not to be involved, which was probably ten times worse than her missing out on a tip-off about the breakup of a Hollywood supercouple.

"Go to dinner," she told Ethan. "Let Nicole take your mind off it." They waved goodbye.

Before backtracking to her car, Zoe paused to watch the skaters at the plaza rink, amused by the contrast of ice skates and sundresses, Christmas trees and dusty palms. By the time she was on her way again, her thoughts had taken a more serious turn, toward the inevitable end of the potion's influence and the end of her story. She didn't want that to also be the end of Shane.

Hailey Valentine was sitting out front of their Spanish white stucco apartment building when Zoe arrived home. She glumly watched Connie sniff at the trunk of a fragrant white oleander bush.

Zoe dropped her bag on the step, keeping an eye on the dog because oleander was poisonous when ingested. "Hi, Hailey. What's up?"

"I hate my stupid school and the stupid prom queens who rule it. And don't tell me it'll be better in college. I don't care about next year. I might not make it to next year." Hailey had plenty of her mother's flair for drama, amplified by adolescent angst.

Zoe plopped down. "I've got a boss breathing down my neck. One of those blondes with perfect silky hair, tailored three-thousand-dollar suits and a wind-tunnel face. I have to hunch at my desk so she won't corner me in my cubicle and rail about demographics."

"Life sucks."

"When it's not blowing."

"But at least you have—" Hailey clamped her mouth shut.

"A convertible?"

"Yeah, that."

"Why don't you make plans this weekend with a friend? I'll let you borrow my car as long as you promise not to drag race down the Boulevard."

Hailey brightened for a moment, then leaned her head on her hands. "I don't want to go out with the girls. They're okay and everything, but y'know."

"So ask a guy out."

"I would rather curl up and die."

"No, you wouldn't. Tell me who you like and I'll tell you how to get him."

"All the cute guys are after the prom queens."

"So maybe you go for someone who's not conventionally cute."

"The losers, you mean. Like I'm such a loser, that's the only kind of guy who'd go out with me."

"That's a pretty negative attitude. I don't know if I'd go out with someone who felt that way."

Hailey scowled. "I heard Mom on the phone to Birgitta. She said you've got a thing going with Mr. Shane."

"So there you are. We've been living side by side for two years and he never thought I'd go out with him, but finally he took a shot anyway." She polished her nails on her shoulder. "Of course, I'm an exceptionally perceptive and open-minded person."

"Does that mean I should call one of the cool guys and hope he knows beauty is only skin-deep?" Hailey gagged.

"You could. But cool guys in high school aren't that ready to break away from the pack. If I were you, I'd look around for the cool guy who's right under my nose. A hottie disguised as a nerd. Or maybe not even a hottie. Just someone who's smart and interesting and can appreciate a girl who doesn't need a tiara to shine."

"No one says *hottie* anymore." Hailey took the dog into her arms. She toyed with the pink rhinestone collar. "Besides, I don't shine."

"You would if you let yourself. You only need some confidence."

"I don't have anything to be confident about."

"There's your artwork." Hailey did computer graphics and fascinating Gothic collages made from bits and pieces she collected at yard sales and junk shops. "One of your collages won second prize in the school art show, right?"

"And you know what won first place? A portrait of Princess Diana painted by one of the prom queens. Technically, it was a good likeness, I suppose, but she was floating on a cloud. Yecchhh."

Zoe laughed, though more sympathetic about the floating-on-a-cloud image than she used to be. "Sometimes there's no getting around it. Life sucks."

"When it's not blowing."

Zoe bumped their shoulders with the girl. "It'll be better next year."

Hailey rolled her eyes. "Sure, when the guys mature and suddenly see how fabulous I am."

"You're the type who'll look better and better as you come into your own. With your great bone structure and those gorgeous green eyes and that wild black hair, ten years from now you'll be a stunner."

"Ten years!"

Zoe laughed hollowly. "They pass before you know it."

"I'm not waiting ten years. I want killer cheek-bones now."

"Killer cheekbones are not for teenage girls. Too intimidating for the fragile adolescent male ego."

Hailey had become distracted, watching as a red Camaro drove by. "Hey, there's that guy again."

"What guy?" Zoe looked up too late from scratching beneath Connie's chin.

"I saw him last night. He was kind of cool but kind of creepy, y'know?"

"How so?"

Hailey shrugged. "He was like a bad boy. He had a short ponytail, an earring and wore shades. Mexican, I think. Sitting in his car, smoking. But old, probably thirty or forty. Mom freaked when I told her he was watching me walk Connie. She was going to call the cops, but he'd driven off by then. I wonder if he lives in the neighborhood."

The girl looked a little too interested for Zoe's peace of mind. She remembered being a teen and seeing older guys watch her on the street in her school uniform. The funny feeling in the pit of her stomach had been new to her.

"If he comes around again, stay away from him, Hailey."

"God, you're as bad as Mom."

Zoe considered mentioning the possible break-in, but decided not to scare the girl unnecessarily. She'd talk to Sara, put her on notice. "Was this guy watching you or the street in general?"

Or their building? Zoe wondered silently. Icy fingers crept along her spine. This was all too coincidental.

"How do I know?" Hailey said grumpily.

Zoe stood. "Let's go in. I need to talk to your mom."

Hailey became alarmed. "Not about me, I hope."

"You know I'm a vault. But I will see if she'll agree to you taking my car this weekend." With one last glance over her shoulder for lurking red Camaros, Zoe followed the girl inside.

11

"WE'LL STALK THE STALKER." Zoe wound her arms around Donovan's waist, trying to pry him from the window. He resisted.

"That sounds like a harebrained scheme. We should go to the police."

"And tell them that someone may have been watching the building so he could sneak in and filch a fake lust potion from my purse, when I left the door to my apartment open while we were having wall-banging sex next door? Oh, yeah, baby. That'll go over big."

"You're only thinking about protecting your story."

"No, I'm thinking of *getting* my story. If it makes you feel better, call it a fact-finding mission. We track down Jag, check things out, maybe figure out how shady his dealings are." She stood on her toes and peered past his shoulder at the street. "See anything?"

"No."

"If the guy that Hailey saw *is* connected to Jag, why would he come back?"

"Because by now he knows for sure that he took the wrong potion."

"And so I can't go home, even though it's right across

the hall and my car is parked out front as obvious as a sombrero on Santa." She moved her breasts against his back. "Do you really believe I'm in danger or are you keeping me here for your own nefarious purposes?" Her hands dropped, framing his hipbones. "If so, you'd better stop looking out the window and start looking at me."

He turned and kissed her, pushing his tongue aggressively into her mouth. She tipped her face up to his, her fingers cool and teasing where they skimmed beneath the edge of his polo shirt. He was hard again. He'd been hard off and on all day, thinking about her. Not only the fiery redhead glory of her naked body or the things she did to make him burn but all the quirks and admirable qualities he'd discovered about her. The apparent color blindness and penchant for pickles. The way she squinted and laughed and wisecracked her way out of sticky emotional moments. Her absolute daring and invincible spirit.

He was becoming sure that the lust potion was one thing and his feelings for Zoe were something else. He had to wonder if he'd been in love with her all along or if it was the sex—sex so amazing it *had* to be life-changing—that had pushed him over the edge.

"So we're agreed?" Zoe smacked her lips. "We stake out Jag's shop and track him to his lair."

He splayed his hands across her bottom, loving the firm curve of flesh that molded to his touch. "What's the point?"

She laughed huskily. "Getting my story."

"You haven't been nagging me for the results of the

chemical analysis." He stretched his neck. He was uncomfortably hot, and the collar was too tight even though it was open.

She lifted the shirt, helping him pull it off over his head. "You'll tell me what you can, when you can."

"What if that means I say nothing?"

Her eyes dimmed a bit, but she looked squarely at him. "I won't ask you to compromise yourself."

He was on the verge of cracking that he'd already done that by gulping the potion, but she deserved respect despite the strange situation surrounding them. "I appreciate that."

"Which is not to say that I won't take any help I can get." She winked.

"I don't know about stalking, but we'll figure something out."

She intertwined his fingers with hers. "A team?"

"A team."

"Now will you take me to bed?"

"My pleasure." He picked her up by the waist and she wrapped her arms and legs around him. Feeling like a macho stud again, he carried her to the bedroom, kicking the door shut behind them. His blood pumped with testosterone, as if his hardwiring had been switched with an action hero's.

More than the potion. He was certain.

DONOVAN CHECKED HIS WATCH. Ten twenty-three in the morning and they were a couple of hundred miles from San Diego, gassing up Zoe's convertible for a journey into the depths of the Mojave Desert. She'd awakened him at some ungodly hour with his laptop open on the bed beside her, telling him to pack for a road trip.

By the blue light of the computer, she'd looked crazy and beautiful, her eyes yellow like a cat's, her skin golden and mottled with freckles, her hair standing on end. All he'd wanted to do was pull her back under the covers and see if a five-a.m. woody was up to the job. But she'd batted his hands away and showed him what a big fish she'd captured through the intrusive databases that put the *net* into Internet: two addresses for Acat Inc.—Jag's company. One on the border in Tijuana, and the other way the hell out in no-man's-land, a town called Castle Springs that was a dot on the map surrounded by a whole lot of nothing.

He'd wanted to go to Tijuana, a hot spot for smuggling.

Which was why they were heading into the Mojave. Zoe had insisted that there had to be a strong reason for Jag to stake out in such a remote location. Despite his reluctance to see her entering a potentially dangerous situation, he'd agreed, but only if he went along. The potential folly of him playing bodyguard was one of those things he was trying not to think too hard about. Like how he'd compromised evidence and his job. And how badly he'd fallen for Zoe. So bad the other worries paled in significance.

"C'mon, what's the holdup? Let's get this rattletrap back on the road," Zoe said, coming out of the gas station with two paper sacks stuffed with junk food. She threw one of them in the trunk along with her leather carryall, then climbed into the shotgun position and upended the other sack into her lap. "Are you hungry? I've got candy bars and energy bars and granola bars and fruit bars…."

Donovan replaced the nozzle and rescued his plastic from the slot on the pump. He placed the card back in his wallet with the folded receipt. Good thing one of them was practical. Before they'd left the city, he'd had an attendant top up the fluids and check the tires, then had stocked the trunk with three jugs of water and an extra ten-gallon can of gas, along with the gear he'd brought along from home, which included a space blanket, a couple of flashlights, flint and a medical kit.

Zoe smiled through a mouthful of orange crumbs when he slid behind the wheel. "I love road trips."

A Pringles cylinder was wedged near the pedals. He fished it out. "Try not to get us killed with your need for grease and sugar, okay?"

She peeled a Three Musketeers. "I bought you the granola bars. And there's trail mix and sugarless gum. You can nibble like a rabbit all the way to Castle Springs."

"Thanks. Did you get liquids?"

"Sure." She handed him a Diet Coke.

He stuck it between his legs and pulled out onto the highway. Maybe he was overly prepared, but they had another eighty miles to go through a barren desert with very few towns along the way.

"What's the plan?" He'd asked versions of the same question ever since they'd started off. Each time Zoe answered differently, probably to get his goat.

"I'll try to get an interview or at least fire off a few pointed questions and see where they land. Maybe photos. I brought a camera." She licked her fingers and stuck them out the window. "And if you ask me the same question again, I'll toss your health food and make you mainline Snickers."

"You're a sugar addict."

She leaned over and put her chin on his shoulder. "Well, you're a *Balam K'am-bi* addict."

"I haven't touched a drop since the fatal swallow."

"Very interesting." She flipped around. "I better make a note." Her cute little butt poked up in the air while she reached behind the seat for her bag. Donovan went cross-eyed. Dirt spit under the passenger-side wheels.

Zoe plopped into her seat and unzipped the bag. "Keep your eyes on the road."

"Then quit distracting me."

"Short attention span. Sweeping arousal." She licked the end of a pencil and wrote in her notebook. "Endless erections."

"Not endless."

She scratched that out. "Constant? No. Frequently renewed erections."

"Did you ever think that I might be addicted to you?"

The tip of lead ground into the page. "For real?"

"This isn't about having a good time."

"You're not having a good time?"

He scanned the dry brown horizon. Except for the rare juniper tree or circling raven, the landscape was lifeless. But he'd biked in canyon country. He knew there was more out there than met the eye. "I'm having a good time."

"In spite of yourself."

"Actually…no. I've always wanted to go on an adventure."

"Then why haven't you?"

"It's not my nature. I'm a planner. And there's my—" He popped the tab on the soda and took a sip. If he wanted their relationship to last, he had to open up. "I have a medical condition. It's not something that affects my daily life, but it's there, at the back of my mind."

Zoe shoveled her things back into the bag, including the scattered packets of half-eaten junk food. She'd gone slightly pale beneath her freckles. "What is it?"

"A heart murmur. I've had it since I was a kid, when the dangers were greater. Now it's nothing." He had a yearly checkup to watch for changes, and that was about it.

"Jeez, Shane. What about the lust potion? What if it had damaged your heart? I mean, you were really, really, *really* charged up."

"I'm fine." He said it with conviction for Zoe's sake, but the old fears weren't so easy to vanquish. His mother had been a worrier, watching him like a hawk, forever cautioning him about the dangers of physical activity despite the doctors who said that a normal level of exercise was beneficial. He was the only kid who'd fought to get *into* gym class.

Eventually his mother's anxieties had sunk in. He'd channeled his interests into books and science and developed a knack for detail work. When college had opened up his world, and he'd excelled in a few criminal-procedures classes taken as electives, an instructor had urged him to apply for the police academy. The heart murmur had nixed that plan. Instead he'd gone back for his Ph.D. and satisfied his curious mind with the kind of work he *could* do. Acquaintances thought dealing with criminal evidence was cool. But he wasn't living *CSI.*

As the miles rolled by, he explained all this to Zoe. She asked a few questions, but for the most part stayed quiet, chewing the inside of her cheek and wiggling her sandaled foot.

"Don't get sympathetic on me," he said. "There's nothing to be concerned about."

"Okay." She peered out at the sky. "It's getting hot. Do you think we should have the top down?"

"Too windy. I might develop a wheeze." She looked alarmed, and he quickly regretted the comment. "That was a joke. You know, without zest."

"I'm sorry about teasing you so much. If I said anything that—"

"Stop, Zoe. Treat me the way you always have."

Her eyes twinkled. "Like a sex toy?"

He laughed, watching the mirror for a vehicle that had been a hundred yards back for the past half hour. "Yeah."

"It's funny how I can hardly remember when I considered you the grouch who lived across the hall."

"That's all I was to you, huh?"

"Don't blame me. I tried to make friends." She

squinted at a road sign. "Whew. Finally. Castle Springs, twenty miles ahead."

"Twenty-nine," he corrected.

"Right." She slid her sunglasses out of her hair and put them on. "Since we're making confessions, here's one of mine. I was a lot like you when I was a kid. Glasses, bookish, isolated, the whole nine yards."

He'd begun to suspect something like that from comments she'd made, as well as the schoolgirl photo in her wallet. "Dorothy Parker lied, you know. Boys do make passes at girls who wear glasses."

"Ha." She tipped down her shades. "Prescription. I wear contacts, too, but the cost adds up, and sometimes I can't afford the new lenses."

"What about the trust fund?"

She aimed a finger outside. "See the desert? My trust fund had almost gone that dry. That's why I'm working at the *Times*."

"Ah."

"If you want the real truth, during most of my twenties, I blew the cash on maintaining a frivolous lifestyle. Well, not all of it. There was a lot—family money and insurance. Some was bilked by a shady accountant, and there's a nice chunk remaining, but I'm saving that as a nest egg. I live on my salary." She looked out the window and added beneath her breath, "Penance."

"What do you mean *penance?*"

She tried to smile. "That's just me being dramatic."

"No, it isn't."

She scraped hair out of her face, taking her time

before answering. "You're right. What I meant is that I've always felt guilty about the way I lost my parents and brother."

"You said it was a car crash. That's not your fault."

"But they were on their way to my graduation."

He glanced in the mirror, then reached over to squeeze her hand. "Zoe. You know you can't blame yourself for a random accident."

"Yes, I know." She sighed. "But emotions aren't always rational."

So he'd learned.

"I ran away from the memories and guilt for a long time. It's only since I've been in San Diego that I've started to grow up." She flicked a hand at him. "Don't say it. I know. I have a lot more maturing to do."

"I wasn't going to say that. I've actually been thinking that you're not half as flighty as you appear." And not half as much an opposite of him as he'd thought. They might have a future after all, even when the potion was completely out of his system.

She laughed. "Not half, huh? If I put on a suit and succeed in making a name for myself like a true Aberdeen, will you bump me up to three-quarters?"

Donovan was heartened by her willingness to share, even if she did it in her typically flippant manner. "Is that why you're dead set on writing a newsworthy lust-potion story? Living up to family expectations?"

"Um, partly. I also have this cockeyed idea that it's time I did something with my life other than report on the migratory habits of celebrities and the people who cater to them."

"I think it's my turn to apologize. I considered you a dilettante and I treated you as one, which must have been belittling at times. I'm sorry for that."

She rubbed her knuckles across her jeans. "So we're even."

He took her hand. "Two wrongs making a right."

CASTLE SPRINGS WAS THE sort of dusty little sun-baked town in which you can't imagine anyone choosing to live. A scruffy cluster of buildings squatted in the dirt and brush, with the only viable businesses catering to passers-through.

"Ought to be easy to find Jag here," Zoe commented. "Where should we ask?"

"The post office. But I don't see one." Shane seemed to be looking toward the highway rather than the town.

She studied the short length of the main street. Every building was the same shade of ochre regardless of its building material. She imagined that the people would be the same—cured brown. Like Jag. "Let's stop here. I'll snag a local and ask. Everybody knows each other in these small towns."

"True enough. I grew up in Solvang, near Santa Barbara."

"Boston."

"A continent apart."

Feeling sort of shy—and astonished that, after what they'd done with each other in the past couple of days, there could be a shred of shyness remaining—she took a quick look at him out of the corner of her eye. "Almost makes me believe in the soul mates concept."

Shane's smile was besotted. "What about the lust potion? That had something to do with us getting together. We might have lived across the hall another five years. I'd have permanent binocular rings around my eyes."

"You're still thinking about my sunbathing habits?" She climbed out of the car. "When this is over, I'm taking you to a topless beach to look at naked boobs until you're immunized."

They walked along the street until an unsuspecting lady in pink capris came out of one of the buildings, balancing a lattice-crusted pie in one hand. Zoe inhaled. "Oh, my gosh. Warm pie. Is that cherry?"

"Sure is. I'm taking it over to the Tick Tock Diner for the lunch rush. Come along if you want a piece." The woman sailed ahead, leading with the pie. She had the weathered brown skin Zoe had expected, but her hair was like bleached cotton candy and her lips and nails were the glossy pink of bubblegum.

Shane caught up in a few strides. "Actually, we're looking for someone. Maybe you can help us?"

"Sure."

"His name is Jag."

The woman slowed to consider. "I know a Panther. He runs the town saloon."

"No, we're looking for Jag. He's about this tall." Zoe leveled a hand near her nose. "Bald. Mexican, I think. In his sixties, I'd estimate. Small and wiry."

"Sorry. That doesn't sound familiar."

"He probably doesn't live here year-round," Shane said.

"Oh, well, snowbirds." The woman shrugged. "There's a whole bunch of them who park RVs and trailers out in the desert."

"Uh, I didn't think of that," Zoe said. "We have an address, but it's only a P.O. box."

"Then you should try the postmaster. He'll be at the Tick Tock about now, on his lunch break."

"Great." Zoe wanted to follow the pie, but Shane stopped her with a touch. She waved the woman off. "We'll catch up."

Shane hustled Zoe around the street corner. "What are you doing?" she demanded.

"I saw a red Camaro turn off the highway. It may have followed us here."

"Followed us?" she shrieked, then clapped a hand over her mouth. "I don't get it. I want to write an article. Just an article. Why are they after me?"

"For some reason, Jag is threatened. I'd guess that's either because you have the potion or because he's figured out where you work." Shane peeked out from behind the building. "Looks like the coast is clear. We can take off if we go now. Or we stick around and hope Camaro man doesn't spot us. What do you choose?"

"I want my story."

"Then we say to hell with the Camaro and go to the diner."

Zoe first took a deep breath, then Shane's arm. "Lead on."

They sauntered to a humble restaurant with a horizontal row of windows facing the road. A giant weather-beaten neon clock loomed over the entrance, looking as if it was one rusted bolt from crashing to the sidewalk. Inside, the counters and tabletops were flecked Formica edged with steel. Turquoise leatherette booths spat wads of stuffing despite heavy applications of duct tape.

A total of six people made up the lunch rush, offering little comfort in numbers.

Shane and Zoe ordered lunch, but neither had much of an appetite. She even passed up the pie. Junk food roiled in her stomach as if an eggbeater had been thrust down her throat.

She swallowed and waved the waitress over. Ten minutes later they had six different suggestions on where to find Jag. No one seemed to know him personally, although there had been vague sightings. For certain, he didn't live in the town proper. One man, a meter reader for the electric company, swore that a house ten or so miles east of town was the place they wanted. "Look for an old wire gate on a dirt road," he said. "You can't see the house from the road, but it's got a big greenhouse attached out back. Can't miss it."

By silent mutual accord, Zoe and Shane departed, leaving thanks and a large tip. On the way back to the car, she expected the Camaro to zoom up, maybe chase them down the sidewalk, but there was no sign of it.

She didn't breathe until they were back in her car. "You drive," she said, although Shane had already taken the wheel. "I think I might have to puke. I don't have the constitution for skulduggery. And nothing big has even happened."

He keyed the ignition. "You're certain you want to keep on?"

"Let's see if we can find the house. I'll decide then how to proceed."

Shane read off the odometer so they could mark the ten miles. Four miles in, she saw his gaze go to the rearview mirror. She whirled in her seat, stretching out the seat belt with one hand. "Are they after us again?"

"I saw a blip on the horizon. The road dips back there. I can't tell for sure."

"So someone follows us. What does that mean?"

"It's a threat. Remember the guy from Jag's yesterday? The bouncer?"

"You think he's Camaro man?" Zoe went over Hailey's description. "I don't know. Hailey said he was cool. A bad-boy type. I'm picturing James Dean, not a bowling ball in combat boots." She gnawed a thumbnail. Spit the torn cuticle out the window. "But he was big and bad. So this could be him."

Shane's knuckles were white on the wheel. He freed a hand to push up his glasses and flexed his fingers. "I could try to lose him by taking a side road."

Zoe was compulsively checking behind them. "We'd kick up a dust cloud."

"And a silver convertible is not exactly the ideal off-road vehicle. Wish we'd rented a Jeep."

"Well, we'd better do something, because there is definitely a car back there. And it's coming up fast."

"Shit," Shane said, and instead of stepping on the accelerator, he slowed to a crawl.

"What are you doing?" Zoe heard her voice doing the shrieky thing again, but she couldn't seem to stop it. "He'll back-end us."

"Hold on." Shane turned the wheel, and they bumped down an incline into flat desert land dotted with scrub and rock outcroppings. He'd done it so smoothly that the dust was minimal, but there wasn't time to get far enough away to completely hide the car. "I'll make a wide turn and get back on the road behind the Camaro. With any luck, looking for us will delay him just enough that we can get a lead back to town." Shane smiled to reassure her. Distractedly she appreciated the attempt. "I'd rather be driving toward town if the threat becomes real."

Zoe had unsnapped her belt so she could follow the other car's progress as their own bumped and jolted across the pockmarked desert. "Damn these sunglasses."

"I brought binoculars. In my duffel."

She reached between the seats and rummaged until she found the binoculars. She put them to her eyes. With one twist, the red Camaro leaped into focus. A plume of dust followed it like rocket fuel.

Two men were inside, both of them large and hulking. And the long, thin object sticking out the passenger window was, without a doubt, the barrel of a rifle.

Zoe squeaked. She gulped, raised and lowered the binoculars, opened her mouth and squeaked again.

"What?" Shane said.

Suddenly her voice returned. Shrill and frantic. "Floor it," she yelled. "They're coming—two of 'em. Coming fast. And they've got a gun."

12

THE THREAT WAS REAL.

Shane jammed his foot on the gas. The convertible bucked and shot forward, crunching through a ridge of desert sage. A huge jolt rocked the vehicle. Zoe slammed into the seat shoulder-first. A bag of cheese puffs exploded. Metal clanged and screeched beneath her feet.

Their undercarriage scraped across a ledge of rock as Shane impelled the car onward through sheer force of will. She grabbed the headrest to pull herself up. "They won't shoot us. They won't shoot us."

There was a loud crack. She yelped and ducked. A fissure appeared in the windshield, casting zigzagged threads like a silver spider web.

"Just a rock," Shane said. "The shot was way overhead. But stay down anyway."

The car was shuddering violently, churning up a sandstorm as they rattled across a rugged terrain where no convertible was meant to go. Zoe coughed, swaying as she inched forward. She braced an arm and rose up high enough to glance over her shoulder. Binoculars were no longer necessary. The Camaro was close. The bottom of her stomach dropped so low the bouncing pebbles could have ticked off it.

"They won't shoot us," she repeated through numb lips.

"No." Shane veered around an immense outcropping, careening for a few terrifying seconds on two wheels. A jumble of rock-strewn hills loomed straight ahead. He slammed on the brakes.

The nose of the car smashed into a boulder. They came to a sudden shuddering stop at a crazy angle, one of the back tires lodged in a chuckhole. Shane flung his door open and was out and dragging Zoe free an instant later. "Run for the hills. Use the rocks for cover."

She ran. He stayed close behind her, urging her on when she stumbled, taking her hand and leading the way as they reached the shelter of the foothills.

A succession of rifle shots rang out. Pebbles and dirt spit in the air only twenty yards away, where they'd vanished among the rocks.

Shane took Zoe in his arms, raggedly telling her they were safe, hidden in a cleft between the red sandstone cliffs.

Yeah, for thirty seconds, she thought.

The crack of another shot reverberated among the rocks. Chips of sandstone rained on their heads.

Thirty seconds and counting.

She dragged in a cutting breath. "We have to go."

They started climbing. It was easy going at first as they picked a path among the boulders on a ground so scoured it was like cement. But soon the route became steep and they had to scramble for handholds, their feet slipping on shale slag as they ascended a treacherous slope. Zoe had escaped with her bag, and they used that as sort of a towrope, linking themselves like mules.

The rocks closed around them, creating an eerie silence broken only by footfalls and harsh breathing. After minutes that seemed like an hour, Zoe collapsed on a wedge of stone at sitting height. "Have to get my breath back."

Shane bent at the waist for a minute, then reached over and tucked her tousled hair behind her ears. "You did great. Stay here and I'll climb a little higher to get a vantage point."

He clambered up the slab. Zoe was too tired to tell him to be careful. She put her head between her knees and spat sand. The speed of her pulse slowed to merely race-the-devil pace. In case she ever had to run for her life again, she was going to invest in a treadmill.

"See anything?" she called softly.

He dropped down beside her. "I couldn't spot their car from here, but I don't think they're following us. Did you get a good look at them?"

"Not really. But I'm pretty sure the bouncer from Jag's was driving. The other guy was taller—that's all I can say. He had the rifle."

She popped up. "Let's go. They might be coming."

Shane hesitated. "Where are we heading?"

"I don't know, but we can't go back."

"They might leave now that they've scared us. Those were warning shots they fired."

"Even so, considering the way we hit that rock, my car's not going any—"

The report of a rifle and a loud *whump*ing sound froze her tongue. An instant later, a double explosion racked the desert, putting a waver in the blue sky above.

Shane went up the slab in a shot, and she followed. From their perch, clinging to the slanted rock face, they saw a billow of black smoke and the lick of flames at the base of the hill.

Zoe moaned. "My car. They killed it."

"Damn. I'm sorry, Zoe."

"Not your fault." She was trying to be as gritty as the inside of her mouth. It was only a car, the last big symbol of her excess. Maybe she was even glad it was gone.

"If I hadn't run us to ground..."

"What could you have done—levitated it over the rocks?" She swiped at her eyes. "How are we going to get out of here now?"

"Look."

A light haze of dust rose in the wake of the red car as it traveled slowly in the direction of the two-lane highway. Zoe reached into the bag still strapped across her chest and gave the field glasses to Shane, then flipped over onto her back and pressed her spine into the flat stone. She didn't want to see.

Shane watched until the car was a speck in the distance, then lay beside her. He stretched out, saying nothing.

They stared at the sky. The sun was still high, the temperature a balmy sixty-five or seventy degrees

Fahrenheit. But night came quickly in the desert, and in December it would be cold. Really cold.

Zoe shivered.

Shane must have been following along the same line of thought. He sat up and checked his watch. "We'd better get moving."

"What if it's a trick? One of them might be waiting down below for us to show."

"We have to take that chance."

She hiked herself up onto her elbows. "Can we make it out here overnight?"

"We'd survive, but it would be cold and uncomfortable." He took off his glasses and spat on the lenses, then used his shirttail to polish them. Only when they were back in place did he look warily at Zoe. "What do you have in mind?"

Sitting cross-legged, she pulled the strap over her head and opened her bag. "I've got food and soda in here. A sweater, too. Unfortunately our jackets were in the backseat."

"Do you have a lighter?"

She dug and came up with a handful of matchbooks from various trendy clubs around town. "Matches."

He took a couple of the packets and tucked them into his shirt pocket. "Wish we had that space blanket I packed."

"In the trunk."

"I was planning for a car breakdown, not this."

She slung an arm around his neck. "I know. And you're my rock. Pardon the expression. I'd probably have sat in the car screaming like a ninny if you hadn't been here."

"I doubt it." He eyed her. "You still want to find Jag, don't you?"

"They've made me mad now. I'm not ready to quit. And, well, we're here, so why not?"

"His place should be close. We were at the eight-point-six mark when the shit hit the fan."

Zoe laughed shortly. "Can we hoof it there before nightfall? I'd at least like to get the lay of the land and snap a few photos."

"I think we'd have to get down out of these hills if we want to get there and still have time to reach the road to hitch a ride back to town." He shook his head. "What am I thinking? Do you have your cell phone?"

She searched the bag fruitlessly. "I had it out. Remember, I had tried calling Hailey to let her know the car might not be available this weekend, then text-mailed her instead." She groaned at the irony. "So it was in the car. What used to be a car. Don't you carry a cell?"

"In my luggage." He patted his pockets. "But I do have this." A Swiss Army knife.

"So are you with me?" When he hesitated, looking ready to pull the plug, she said, "You wanted an adventure. This is an adventure. C'mon, live a little."

"I was thinking James Bond. Something with martinis and bikinis, not explosions and bouncers."

She couldn't believe he'd made her laugh at a time like this. "Let's try it. We don't have anything to lose."

"Except ourselves."

"We don't have that far to go. We can't possibly get lost."

Shane surveyed their position. "Not if we stick to the edges of these rocks, keeping the road on our north. That'll mean a lot of climbing in and out among the boulders. Are you game?"

She smiled bravely. "Let me eat a candy bar first." If she could swallow with the stink of burning metal and gas clogging her throat.

THE SUGAR RUSH DIDN'T last long. Within twenty minutes her ankles were rubber bands from climbing the uneven surfaces. By the forty-minute mark her calves were cramping. She stopped to rub at the muscle, wondering if Shane, souped up by the remnants of the lust potion, was doing better.

He looked back. "You're going to have start bike riding with me."

Her lip curled. "I despise exercise. My official slogan. When this is over, I'm printing T-shirts."

"We can take a break."

"Great. Thanks." In case he hadn't noticed, she was already on one.

Shane had removed his top shirt and tied it around his head like a Bedouin. Instead of looking spent, he seemed tanner and fitter, as if the rugged challenge had invigorated him. The light sprinkling of stubble on his jaw only made him look more attractive, while she was a sweaty, stinking mess. Life wasn't fair. Except that she got to look at him, instead of vice versa.

She took the soda he offered from her stash, having surrendered her bag to him ten minutes into their journey. The lukewarm liquid was a miracle to her parched throat. She had to force herself not to gulp down the entire can at once.

"Do you want a snack?"

"Not now." Her stomach churned every time she thought about the rifle shots, even though Shane insisted they hadn't been meant to kill. Persisting in finding Jag's lair was probably one of her dumber moves, considering. If Shane had shown signs of refusing, she'd have capitulated in an instant.

But that was her indulgent side talking. Aberdeens weren't supposed to quit so easily. On her trips to Africa, Zoe's mother had thrived under the much rougher conditions.

Zoe dug deep, hoping to find some of that gumption inside herself. This wasn't only about her family's memory now. She wanted to impress Shane, too. Her colleagues were running a poor third, and the Hollywood power brokers she'd hoped to entice weren't even on the radar screen.

She stopped with the soda can at her lips. "You're not having any?"

"We only have a couple more."

She gave him her can, feeling guilty. "There's a little left."

He drank it down. The swallowing movement of his throat was an erotic thing. She looked at the trickle at the corner of his mouth and wanted to lick it off.

She plucked her sunglasses from the neck of her tank and put them on. Even the sweat patches on his T-shirt and the dirty knees of his khakis were getting her hot. She fanned the back of her neck, where her sensitive skin had been exposed to the sun by the haphazard bun she'd fashioned with a strip torn from the hem of Shane's shirt. Her sexual appetite had lost all sense of propriety.

She looked up to find him watching her with his eyes all broody. Her heart beat a little faster. She clutched her thighs to keep from making inappropriate advances. This was no time for the potion to kick in.

"It seems like we've been walking forever." She wiped her brow. Her dusty jeans bore two sweaty palm prints. "How much farther? Are you sure we haven't overshot Jag's road?" Although they hadn't been certain they were on the right track in the first place, being chased by gunfire had more or less settled that question.

"Jag's road is supposed to run north-south, give or take a few degrees. We *have* to cross it."

"But when? I know I'm a big weenie compared to you, but I'm pooped."

"We should be almost there. The tough going makes you feel like you've traveled five times as far as you have." Shane looked at his watch. "It's past three. If you're up to it, I'm thinking we should cut across the last of these hills. That should bring us right into Jag's backyard."

"More climbing?" If they ever reached it, the sand and relatively even terrain of the desert floor would seem like paradise. Except that there'd be no cover. She wasn't ready to give up her cover. "I can do it."

IF DONOVAN EVER WENT mountain trekking again, he was taking Zoe no matter what. Watching her push herself past the limit and then further still was a lesson he'd never forget. He'd known intellectually that he'd played his life too safe, but now he felt it in his gut, as well.

Zoe was a fighter, whether or not she knew it. He loved her for that.

And for her damned cute butt, too.

That cute butt was currently lodged against his shoulder as he helped lower her to a level surface off the giant red boulder they'd just surmounted.

She swatted at her jeans, then froze. "Shh. Listen. Do you hear water?"

"Water? I doubt it. There might be a stream, but generally they dry up in the winter months."

"The town *is* called Castle Springs. Maybe we just climbed into the castle." She held up a finger for silence. "I definitely hear water."

He watched her scramble off in the opposite direction they ought to be taking and slide on the seat of her jeans down a slope of limestone. "Zoe?"

"I can smell it," she called, sounding almost giddy.

"All right. We'll check it out. But we shouldn't go far off course." He traced her route, feeling abashed at how quickly he'd fallen back into his rut. Changing old habits would take some time.

"Sweet mercy," he heard Zoe say from the entrance to a crevasse. "I've found heaven on earth."

Heaven turned out to be a stream that cut through the

rocks like a skinny green snake. It was the kind of stream that would foam up into a raging current if there was a flash flood but for now was trickling harmlessly barely six inches deep.

Zoe had squatted and was splashing the water on her face and neck. She grinned broadly, dripping from the nose and chin. "It's cold. I can't believe how good it feels."

"Don't drink any."

"I won't. But I want to."

"There are parasites and germs."

She leaned over and sank her hands up to her wrists, her shoulders relaxing at the simple pleasure of the wash of cold water. He knelt beside her, dropped the bag and followed suit.

The icy chill was a rousing shock. He let out a boyish shout and scooped handfuls onto his face.

Zoe leaned in and kissed him. "Nice, isn't it?" she said against his mouth. Her lips were firm and cold, her tongue teasing him with its velvet warmth.

He cupped her jaw. Closed his eyes. Drank thirsty kisses.

She murmured with pleasure. "I want to see where the stream goes."

He sucked gently at her lower lip before releasing her. He was on the verge of saying that exploring was a waste of time and effort, but for once he wanted to do the non-sensical thing. "We can go a short way."

The reward was worth the delay. They followed the stream, straddling it with their feet placed on narrow ledges cut into the stone walls. The passageway opened up within twenty yards, to a small pool sheltered by an overhang of rock. Glistening tracks lined one of the vertical walls, where a waterfall would appear during the rainy season.

"I could almost jump in," Zoe said, standing on the edge of the deep green pool.

"You'd freeze."

"Better than being hot and sweaty."

He raked his hands through dampened hair. "No, it's not. Not with night coming and the temperature dropping…"

He shut up. She'd removed the sweater she'd put on to prevent sunburn, then stripped her tank top. Now she was stepping out of her shoes, sliding off her jeans. Which left her clad in a thong and a smile.

"You're crazy. You'll get hypothermia." It was his duty to warn her.

"I'm not jumping in." She scooted down onto a shallow dip, where the pool lapped at a shelf of flat, wet rock. "I'm bathing."

She splashed a little, then sat with her legs submerged for about two seconds. "Yikes, that's cold." A shiver rippled through her. "But invigorating. Come on, Shane. Take off your shirt. Get a little crazy."

He unlaced his boots.

Zoe kicked her feet in the pond like a playful child in a wading pool.

"Nut." He rolled up his pants, sat on a dry spot nearby and stuck his feet into the water. The instant chill was bracing but welcome. He took off his shirt and freshened up, keeping an eye on Zoe as she hugged her legs, folded under her chin. The reflection looking back at her from the emerald pool was a naked sprite, painted in watery green.

She climbed out, shivering. Her breasts were ivory, almost luminescent, tipped by strawberry nipples drawn into tiny buttons.

"I've had enough."

"C'mere, I'll warm you." He stood and gave her a full-body hug.

She danced against him, teeth chattering. "I have to get clothes on."

"Dry off first." He chafed her skin. "The sun's already dropping. You don't want to be walking around in damp jeans."

"Dry off with what?"

"Use my shirt." He pulled it off his head and rubbed her down, trying not to think about her pearly skin or the curve of her back or how touching the sweet spot on the inside of her thighs always made her spread them with a sigh.

"My thong's wet." She broke away to step out of it and into her jeans. The way she hopped a little and wiggled as the denim skimmed past her hips drove him wild.

She left the pants unzipped but covered her breasts with her hands. "Uh-oh. You've got that look again."

"Sorry. Now's not the time, I know."

"Count to ten," she suggested.

One—her smart mouth that tasted so good.

Two—the shallow dimples that punctuated her fine ass.

Three—the orgasms he'd given her last night.

Four—the freckles that dotted her right breast.

Five—

The hell with five. He stepped closer. "Just a kiss," he said, but a minute later he was lost in the warmth of her mouth and thinking that he could stroke her breasts without going any further. And five minutes after *that,* his hand was inside her jeans and he was fingering the sensitive nub hidden there and watching her lashes flutter as her knees went out and she sagged against him.

Holding her up with one arm, he wrapped her sweater around her, lifted and carried her to the sun-splashed slab of slanted rock. He'd intended to leave her there, but she opened her arms and gave a welcoming murmur, and he found himself bending closer, kissing and caressing every quivering inch of her. She moved sensuously against the rock, melting into his touch as he teased her nipples with his thumbs and then his teeth and tongue.

Their passion slipped past the turning point without either of them noticing. Making love beneath the sapphire sky seemed entirely appropriate.

He kissed her breasts. "Is the stone uncomfortable?"

"No, it's warm." She spread her hands over his chest. "So are you."

He eased between her legs with his feet still planted on solid rock, bracketing her shoulders with his forearms. His fingers twined in her hair and he kissed her sweet mouth, their tongues playing advance and retreat.

He nuzzled her neck. "We should be moving on."

"Five minutes. Call on the power of *Balam K'am-bi*."

"Only five minutes?"

"Balam K'am-bi," she chanted, stretching beneath him, then curling upward against his erection, nudging him with the press of her hips. *"Balam K'am-bi."*

"Balam K'am-bi," he whispered, and damn if he didn't feel the drumbeat pounding through his bloodstream. It was doping and energizing at once, narrowing his focus and blowing open his brain.

"Take me." Zoe touched his face. "Love me."

He slid a hand inside her jeans. She writhed at the first touch, so hot and wet and open. He wasted no time in retrieving one of the condom packets he'd stuffed into his pants pocket when he'd been preparing to the nth degree.

After tugging her jeans lower and cradling her bottom, he entered her slowly, bending his knees into the slant and thrusting with his hips as she met him, enfolding and igniting him with her sweet liquid fire.

A hawk circled overhead with a languid flap of its wings. Shane squeezed his eyes shut, surrendering to the careening agony of sensations as the savage rhythm lifted them higher and higher. He gasped at the tightening vise of Zoe's climax and felt the aching knot inside him burst into the burning geyser of his own release.

13

"THE LAIR OF THE JAGUAR," Zoe intoned in a sepulchral voice to combat her nerves. With her chin resting on a chiseled ledge of shale, she studied what they presumed to be Jag's home away from home. The house was not impressive—a low stucco building with scrubland for a front yard. There were several vehicles parked randomly out front, including the dusty red Camaro.

"Heh." Shane raised the binoculars. "That greenhouse…"

"Suspicious, isn't it?"

"Maybe Jag grows orchids in his spare time."

"I'll bet."

It was early evening, and already they'd lost the light as the sun dropped down behind the hills at their backs. Long purple shadows stretched across the open space between them and the house. Birds flicked and twittered through the dusk. A wintry wind whipped up eddies of dirt and gravel. Zoe pulled her sweater closer to her body, wishing for the jackets they'd left in the car. The lighthearted warmth that had segued to a steamy encounter at the hidden pond seemed a hundred miles away.

Shane passed her the binoculars. "Okay, boss. What now?"

"We look for evidence." She'd already snapped a few photos with her digital camera, but that was proof of nothing. The license plate numbers she'd recorded might yield a bonus.

"With that many cars out front? No way."

"But we've come all this way. And I'm dying to see what's in the greenhouse." She focused the glasses on the structure that protruded from the back of the house. Homemade, she presumed. Raw posts and planks made up the framework, which was wrapped in heavy opaque plastic sheeting shadowed by plant shapes. A tin stovepipe stuck out of the roof at the back end. White smoke rose in spirals that flattened in the wind.

There *had* to be something valuable growing inside.

Shane hunkered down behind the rock and tore the cellophane off a package of peanut butter crackers. "Say I agreed. How are we going to get across the scrub? You can't hide very well behind a creosote bush."

"We wait until dark."

"Do you know how cold it'll be by then? Near freezing."

She picked out one of the crackers. "But we're stuck here either way. If we sneak up to the house, we could steal one of the cars to make our getaway."

"You're turning into a real maverick." He considered. "Still, that might not be a bad idea, if we're willing to be chased all the way to Castle Springs. I'm not keen on the option, but there doesn't seem to be much traffic on the highway. Even if we left now, we could be hitching for hours." He shrugged. "All right. I'm in."

She blinked. "You are?"

"But we don't try any funny business. Sneak up, peek in the greenhouse, borrow a ride. That's it. How you get your story after that is up to you." He took her hand. "As long as it doesn't involve any heroics, which I'll kick your butt for even thinking about."

"Agreed."

He shook his head. "I can't believe you talked me into that."

"Didn't I tell you? The power of *Balam K'am-bi* knows no bounds."

"Sort of like the power of redheads."

An hour later they'd climbed down out of the rocks and were crouched behind the creosote. Shane surveyed with the binoculars. Lights had come on in the house, but the only sign of the occupants was the occasional silhouette in a window. "We've got a Joshua tree to our right. Let's head for that."

Staying low, they scurried for their next cover. Zoe sucked in a shocked breath when an iguana darted out in front of them and disappeared into the creosote. "My heart is pounding like crazy," she whispered when they ducked behind the tree.

"Mine too." Shane used the glasses again. "This is where it gets risky. Between here and that propane tank near the house, our only possible cover is the blowout."

"What's a blowout?"

He guided her hand, aiming a finger to show her the

way. "See that depression in the earth? It's caused by wind erosion."

"You mean the ditch. Yeah, that'll save us."

There was no movement near the house. But they were close enough now to hear the sounds of talk and laughter, the blare of a sporting event on TV. "On three," Shane whispered.

Zoe took off at two. She'd never been good at waiting around.

They were almost past the house when the front door opened, releasing a burst of light and loud voices. A bulky man stepped out, calling over his shoulder to someone inside the house. Keys jingled in his hand.

It was the driver of the Camaro—the bouncer from Jag's.

"Dive," Shane said in a hoarse whisper, and Zoe dived facedown in the dirt of the scooped-out ditch. He landed half on top of her with a thump.

The jingling stopped. "Who's there?"

They froze. Zoe kissed the ground, breathing through her nose in sharp puffs of air that stirred the sand. She could feel Shane's heart against her shoulder blade. *Tha-dunk. Tha-dunk.*

Out in the desert, a coyote yelped.

"Trouble?" asked a second voice. "You think they're still out there?"

"Naw," the first man said. "Not a chance. We scared 'em good with that bonfire."

Zoe turned her head and Shane touched his mouth to her cheek. *Don't move,* he mouthed.

Footsteps thudded toward them and her stomach clutched tight, but then came the creak of a car door opening. Headlights sliced through the darkness, lighting the lip of the blowout. The engine roared. She clawed deeper into the sand. The car reversed in a half-circle and drove away.

Zoe opened her eyes and waited for the slam of the front door before she huffed, "How could I move when you're on top of me?"

Shane exhaled into her hair. "You never had trouble before."

They waited, listening and shivering, until Zoe's hands were numb with cold. "This is too dangerous," Shane said. "Let's just go for a car and get out of here while we have the chance."

"No. Please." A stubborn refusal to run had ignited inside her. Not this time. Her reasons were bigger than a news article. This was about the rest of her life.

Shane gripped her. "Zoe, don't jeopardize it. I won't let you risk yourself."

She wouldn't listen to his plea. Without warning, she lifted herself up and ran silently for the greenhouse, circling around to the back of it. She pulled up, breathing hard. The scent of wood smoke was sharp in the air.

Sensing Shane behind her, she put out her hand. "Give me the knife. I'm going to slice through this plastic."

Instead of the knife, a hand closed around her wrist. She whirled.

A broad-chested wall of man towered above her, all black shadow except for a flash of teeth and the gleam of a small gold hoop earring. "You're a very stupid girl," he said in what she believed was a Latino accent. "You should have listened to Heriberto and stayed away."

For a second, something in the man's face or voice—a barely discernible hesitation—gave Zoe hope that he would simply send her away.

And then Shane attacked out of nowhere, wielding the knife and a bloodcurdling scream.

The tall man whipped out a leg and knocked the weapon away with one blow. It went flying into the darkness. Zoe tried to yank her arm away so she could go after the knife, but the man held her as easily as if she were a rag doll while he fended off Shane's fists with a massive forearm.

With a feral growl, Shane rained blows on Zoe's captor. An uppercut caught the man by surprise, snapping back his head. He let out a curse, released Zoe and launched himself at Shane full force. The two men collided like mountain goats and fell to the ground in a tangle of flying punches and flailing legs.

Zoe had been flung aside. She crawled in the direction of the knife, only to be hauled up by her scruff by another man. An alarm had been raised in the house. Doors banged. Men shouted.

Jag appeared out of the darkness, carrying a flashlight. He shined the light in Zoe's face. "You again."

She struggled against her captor, a younger man in a cowboy hat who laughed and caught her around the waist, lifting her a few inches off the ground. He smelled like beer and compost.

Jag redirected the light. "Chac?"

The black-clad man sat astride Shane's prone body, securing his wrists with a plastic zip strip. He rose gracefully in an impressive display of honed muscle, not even breathing hard. "Caught these two lurking near the greenhouse."

Two other men stood nearby, one wizened like Jag, the other almost a carbon copy of the bouncer—Heriberto's brother, Zoe guessed—except for a narrow stripe of black Mohawk that bisected his bald head and ended in a lank ponytail.

Shane's head lifted. She saw by the flicker of his eyes that he was also counting.

Five against two. Six if Heriberto returned.

They were done for.

"Look at it this way," Zoe said to Shane without moving her mouth. "We got to see inside the greenhouse."

"Is it all that you expected?" He sat on the rough wood-plank floor with his back to her, hands and feet bound by the zip strips. They'd gone easier on Zoe. Only her hands were tied. Chac had wrapped a length of twine around her wrists, then wound and knotted the ends around the support post of one of the greenhouse tables.

She glanced up at the jungle of greenery. "It's like a rain forest in here."

"Exactly." The greenhouse dripped with moisture and humidity. Foliage glistened from the constant light sprinkle of the suspended watering system. A wood stove against the far wall pumped out heat at a subtropical level. "I'm no expert, but I'd say most of these plants are rain-forest varieties."

"And Jag grows them to make the lust potion," she whispered. "Could they be illegal in this country? He might smuggle them over the border to avoid customs."

"Possibly. Except…"

"What?"

"I've analyzed the potion, remember? The plant extracts weren't harmful." Shane paused. "The only unusual substance in the mix was an animal pheromone."

She pressed against him, telling him without words that she appreciated his trust. "Then why the secrecy, growing this stuff out here in the middle of nowhere?"

"They could be manufacturing more than the lust potion."

"I wonder." Zoe went silent. He felt her working her arms, trying to saw the twine against the post.

He touched a bare patch of skin at the small of her back. "Keep an eye out." She had a better view into the house than he, through a door that had been left half open. After trussing them up and dumping them in the greenhouse, Jag and his cohorts had returned to the house. Their voices rose and fell. Snatches of the discussion suggested that they were worried about the "heat" and debating what to do with their captives. Cesar, Heriberto's Mohawked brother, was in favor of depositing their torched bodies in the burned-out car.

Zoe made a small noise of triumph. "I'm snagged on a splinter. If I can use the sharp point to slice through—"

She snapped her mouth shut as the man they'd called

Chac walked in. He was the most intimidating of the lot, but Shane was pleased to see a dark bruise swelling on the man's jaw. He wasn't a fighter by any stretch, but when Zoe had been captured, he'd unleashed his potion-adrenalized inner beast. Unfortunately *Balam K'am-bi*'s power *did* have bounds.

There was silence from the house as Chac stomped up to them. He gave Shane a vicious kick in the thigh with his combat boots. "You two. Keep your mouths shut."

Shane grunted in pain.

Inside, the talk resumed.

Chac went to the wood stove and stocked it with short lengths of pinyon and mesquite. On the way back, he paused beside them, his cruel gaze crawling over every detail. Shane was almost certain the man had noticed Zoe's attempts to break free, yet he said nothing.

A distraction was called for. Shane spoke in a hushed tone. "We were wondering what kind of plants these are."

The man showed his teeth like a shark. "Poisonous."

Zoe whispered, too. "From Mexico?"

"The Yucatan."

"To make *Balam K'am-bi?*"

Chac raised an eyebrow.

"You don't want to kill us," Zoe said confidently. A glare from Chac hushed her.

He glanced into the kitchen of the house, where the other men sat around a table with drinks and smokes, not paying any particular attention to the greenhouse as they rummaged through the bag they'd confiscated from

Zoe. Her damp, wadded thong made an appearance, to great sport. Cesar ripped open the last bag of chips.

Chac gestured with a flick his head. "Death Camas." A lilylike plant in a terra-cotta pot. A string of names came in quick succession. "Lantana. Cowhage. Rosary Pea."

Chac looked significantly at Shane. "Manicheel." He indicated a bushy tree that had grown almost to the sagging roof from its large boxed container. "Poisonous. All of it. Even the water dripping from the leaves."

Shane nodded, calculating how he could use the knowledge to rescue Zoe. That the Mexican was hinting at Jag's illegal schemes—which might lead to the city's recent rash of poisonings—was secondary.

"Chac?" Jag called. "You with us?"

An unpleasant grin twisted the man's lips. "Coming." He closed the door as he left the greenhouse, cutting off their view into the kitchen. And vice versa.

"Try to break free," Shane urged.

Zoe wriggled closer to the post and stabbed her binding against the splinter. "What was that about?"

"I have a feeling Chac isn't really one of the gang."

"Then he should have let us go outside," she whispered furiously, making frustrated sounds as she tried to cut through the twine.

"He might have. If I hadn't attacked and made that impossible."

"Are you thinking what I'm thinking—about the poisonings that have happened lately? What if Jag is selling potions that cause more than lust?"

"Shhh." Shane inched forward and used his feet to drag a plant saucer out from beneath the tables, where rolls of burlap, bags of compost, stakes and shovels had been stashed. With another nudge, the saucer was positioned beneath the dripping leaves of the manicheel tree.

"It's fraying." Zoe whimpered. "But the splinter broke."

"Snap the twine. You can do it."

She hunched her shoulders and wrenched with all her might.

The twine broke.

She turned to Shane, fumbling for his wrists. "You have to cut the zip strips. Find something quick. But don't let them see."

She darted about, looking through the jumble of gardening items for a knife or nippers. Grabbing up a large pair of shears, she inserted one of the broad rusty blades between his hands and cut through the zip strip, then freed his feet.

He knelt and lifted the saucer. Only a small amount of water had been collected.

"What are you doing? Let's just go."

"What if the keys aren't in the cars? We might not make it. We have to incapacitate them. Get a pot or a cup."

Zoe paled, but she followed his direction and found a small plastic pot rimmed with dirt. He poured the poisonous water into it. "If they come after you, throw the water in their eyes. It'll blind them."

She inspected the meager amount. "Then we need more."

They tipped the branches, catching the trickling

moisture in their containers. "Don't let the leaves touch your skin," he cautioned.

"This is a crazy plan."

"Not when Chac is on our side."

"You're sure?" she whispered. Her eyes were like gold coins. "How come?"

"I don't know."

She bit her lip. "Chac is a Mayan name. A god, I think. I researched Mayan culture for my article."

Every second they used increased the risk of being caught. They each had an inch of water at most, but it would have to be enough.

"Now we leave," Shane whispered as he picked up a shovel in his free hand. They moved silently to a side door that hung crookedly in its frame, locked only by a hook and latch.

A shout brought them up short. "Hey!" Cesar had widened the door and stuck his head into the green-house. "They're loose. Grab the guns."

Hell. Guns. Shane flung the water from his saucer at Cesar's face as Chac and the other younger man burst in.

Cesar swabbed his eyes. "Water? That's all you got?" Suddenly his belly laugh was cut short. He blinked and rubbed his eyes. "Shit. That stings." He let out a howl of pain and lurched blindly at Shane, who swung the shovel at his head. Cesar went down with a boom.

The man who'd earlier yanked Zoe off her feet by her hair had run forward. She splashed him with the remaining water, but he kept coming. She dodged out of the way. Shane swung the blade of the shovel at the back of the man's knees, and he buckled, clutching at the makeshift table of potted plants as he fell.

Cesar rolled on the floor, groaning and clawing at his face.

Chac stood by, his arms folded across his chest, his face expressionless.

Shane grabbed Zoe's hand and pulled her through the door as Jag arrived in the greenhouse, jabbering in Spanish. They heard Chac say with lethal calm, "Don't worry. I'll get them back."

There was still the fifth man, who might have a gun. Shane paused at the corner of the house and peered around a small propane tank. They were clear.

Zoe ran to the closest car and cupped her hands over the window. "No keys."

They went to the next, a black Blazer. The front door of the house banged open and Chac appeared in the square of light. A rifle was propped against his hip.

"Crap," Zoe said and rattled desperately at the car door handle.

Chac stepped forward and tossed Shane a set of keys.

Zoe stopped rattling. "Who are you?"

"A tool of revenge," Chac said with a ghost of a grin.

Shane had unlocked the door and swung it open. He boosted Zoe up into the front seat. "I want to talk to you about *Balam K'am-bi,*" she called to Chac.

He shook his head. "Never heard of it."

There was a flurry of movement inside the house. Chac cocked the gun. "Go. *Now.*"

Shane slid behind the wheel and started the engine.

Zoe leaned across him, trying to get to the window. She pounded the glass. "What about Jag?"

Chac's face darkened. "He'll be taken care of."

Shane revved the engine and the back wheels spun in the dirt before catching. The Blazer lunged forward into the night.

In the mirror he saw Chac raise the rifle as Cesar stumbled out of the house. He raged, but Chac easily held him off with one hand pushed against the man's barrel chest.

They sped down a rutted trail to the gate.

A gunshot cracked behind them.

Zoe ducked. "Not again."

"It's okay. He's not shooting toward us this time."

She popped up. "Why—"

A boom sounded behind them. She twisted in the seat, her mouth dropping open as a small fireball blossomed with dancing orange flames.

Shane's gaze flicked to the mirror. "The propane tank. The house'll go up next. Then the greenhouse."

"I don't understand."

The headlights shone on a wire lattice gate, padlocked. On either side, barbed wire stretched into the black night. Shane applied the brakes and the Blazer fishtailed to a halt. He glanced back at the house as flames crept along the roof. "I'm guessing that Chac was sent to put a stop to Jag's operation. Smuggling, poisons, the potion—all of it. He never intended to hurt us."

"But if it was him who broke into my apartment and took the potion—"

"He was only obeying orders. Probably didn't want to blow his cover as one of the henchmen. Until we forced the issue."

"I wonder." Zoe sighed. "Now we'll never know for sure about the lust potion."

"It's the pheromones," Shane said, and she blinked at him with shiny eyes. His voice grated in his throat. "Put on your seat belt."

"You said that before, in the greenhouse. Animal pheromones. But what kind?"

"What kind do you think?" Shane put the Blazer into gear and stepped on the gas. "Jaguar, of course."

Zoe gripped the dashboard. She was laughing as they tore through the gate.

14

"SEX," BARBARA BITTERMAN PROCLAIMED, brandishing a folded copy of yesterday's newspaper in over-the-top triumph. "Gunfire. Poison. Explosions."

She dropped the paper and took Zoe by the shoulders. "I want more. Our *readers* want more. You must give it to them."

"But the police—"

Bitterman shook Zoe. She flung her hands high. "Never mind the police. Get me the entire story."

Perhaps realizing that she'd exhibited enough emotion to put lines on her face, the editor stopped gesticulating and tugged down the short fitted jacket of her white cashmere wool suit. "We'll run the full story in this Sunday's magazine section."

"I can't—"

"Next Sunday then." Bitterman thrust out an arm, pointing to the door. "Go. Write."

Zoe exited. Clearly she was not going to be able to finish a sentence to explain that the police were saying that although the poisoning cases were still under investigation, there'd be no arrests concerning the alleged lust potion. Even pinning the illegal trade in poison on Jág and his cohorts was iffy, considering that the best evidence had burned to the ground when Chac had lit up Jag's lair. And Jag, along with his accomplices, had mysteriously disappeared into the desert before the fire trucks had arrived.

Zoe scanned the newsroom for Kathryn as she descended the steel staircase. She'd planned to expand on the story even before Bitterman's edict. Once the local news stations had reported that Jag's shop in the Gaslamp Quarter remained open, she'd known she had to return. But she didn't want to go alone. Being shot at and having your car set on fire tended to give a person the heebie-jeebies.

Kathryn was in her office, tip-tapping at her keyboard.

Zoe threw herself into a chair. "Read any good books lately?"

"That depends on your definition of good. Ever since I reviewed *Bound in Brasilia*, I've got erotica coming out my ears."

"Coming out your ears? Heh."

Kathryn turned a sharp eye on Zoe. "You don't seem your normal zippy self. I thought you'd be thrilled having your story on the front page."

"Oh, no, that's great. Super. I am thrilled." Zoe examined a springy lock of hair. "Except now Barbie wants an in-depth account and I'm not sure how to go about it. I managed to skim over any mention of *Balam K'am-bi* in the article since the story focused on the fire and my adventures in the desert. But now I'll have to give the inside scoop. She wants sex. Lots of juicy tell-all sex."

Kathryn's brows lifted. "Since when have you had a problem with that?"

"I suppose…" *Spit it out, Zoe. It's only the end of your world as you know it.* She licked her lips. "I suppose it's different because I kinda went and fell in love with Shane."

Kathryn crowed. "I knew it!"

Zoe rubbed her eyes. The contacts were annoying her. Her trusty sunglasses had been lost during their escape, probably melted in the blaze. Now she had to look at the world without dusk-colored lenses, and it'd turned out everything seemed different. Brighter. Lighter. Happier. More promising.

She didn't have to exaggerate anymore.

"Are you crying?"

"Hell, no." Zoe sniffed. "It's my contacts."

Kathryn's smile was sympathetic. "There's nothing wrong with having a heart, you know."

"I miss the old me. The wild, carefree, don't-give-a-damn me."

"Trust me." Kathryn's gaze swept Zoe's dress and accompanying jewelry—a circus-tent shift of citrus stripes and glitter-encrusted bangles. "The old Zoe hasn't gone anywhere."

Kathryn was right. Zoe told herself to quit sniveling and get investigating. She counted silently, and by the time she got to ten, her jaw was set. She could do this.

"One of the problems is, how am I going to tell the tale of the lust potion? No one who hasn't used the stuff will believe a word of it."

Kathryn's head tilted. "You know, maybe that doesn't

matter. We know there's proof—because *we're* the proof—but as far as the readers are concerned, they only want to be intrigued, enchanted, involved. Swept away by the mystery and romance of it all."

Zoe grinned. "You've been reading too much erotica."

Kathryn stroked her cheek. "Even better—I've been living it."

Me, too, Zoe said to herself, briefly closing her eyes as she thought of the past night with Shane. *Every* night with Shane. While it was true that he'd had a bigger dose of the potion than anyone else, it seemed to her that the effects should have worn off by now. If they were ever going to wear off.

She sat up straighter. "Kath? Come to Jag's with me."

"Won't it be closed?"

"Probably. But I want to see for sure."

"What about the men, the, uh—"

"The brothers, Cesar and Heriberto?"

"What if they're there?"

Zoe thought of Cesar cackling over the torching of their car—and potentially their bodies. "We'll need muscle." She wished for Shane, who would first scoff at being called muscle and then threaten to tie her to the bed to keep her safe…and safe-sexed. He was apt, she'd learned, at accomplishing both objectives.

Chac, of course, was gone. Their benevolent grim reaper.

That left one option—a man whose wit and charm tended to slay opponents long before muscles were called for. But fortunately he had those, too.

Zoe looked at Kathryn. "Let's take Ethan."

"ISN'T THIS WHERE WE STARTED?" Ethan rolled up the sleeves of his white button-down shirt. His hair was rumpled and a thin striped tie hung loose around his neck.

"Don't take the muscle thing too seriously," Zoe said. "I once blinded a muscleman with firewater."

Kathryn used her height to peer past Zoe's head at Jag's shabby storefront. "Good reason to be cautious."

"I think we're safe," Ethan said drily.

A sign in the window read Going Out of Business. A steady stream of customers came and went, drawn by the curiosity that Zoe's *Times* article had provoked and other media outlets had fanned into flames.

"Apparently half of Southern California needs a bottle of counterfeit lust potion in their Christmas stocking," Ethan said. "Let's get inside while we still can."

They entered the shop, pushing through the crowd around the cash register. Zoe glimpsed a beautiful young Latina behind the counter, a woman with shining hair and dark, gentle eyes. "I can't see. Is there someone else…?"

Kathryn craned her neck. "A little brown woman who looks like a crow."

"Shit." Zoe ducked. "That's the lady Heriberto called Tia. His aunt. Possibly Jag's wife. She's a viper."

"I'll take her out for you." Ethan jabbed a fist and nearly took off a baked blonde's baseball cap. She snarled, clutching a toy poodle with one hand and a bottle of potion with the other.

"The vipers are everywhere," Ethan said out of the side of his mouth.

"Don't laugh. You might have to stick up for me if they recognize—"

A screech cut through the customers' chatter. "There she is—the redheaded *bruja*."

The crowd stirred, moving away from the register. Tia was trying to climb over the counter, fire in her eyes.

The young woman who'd been been making change grabbed Tia around the waist. She coaxed the woman toward the corner of the shop, finally shoving her through the curtain into the back room. She hissed Spanish, then whipped around and snapped the drape shut.

Zoe had approached. "I'm Zoe Aberdeen."

"I know who you are." The young woman pinned the curtain to the door frame with both hands, using her weight to keep Tia trapped on the other side. "We all know who you are."

"Where's Jag?" Zoe asked.

The woman shook her head, her gaze dark and unwavering. From behind the fabric barrier came a torrent of Spanish invective, possibly in a Mayan dialect, if the anthropology professor that Zoe had been speaking to was correct. According to her, the jaguar lust potion *Balam K'am-bi* was a legendary mystery, considered so rare and potent it was only whispered of among a particulary obscure tribe in the Yucatan. Facts were as difficult to gather as mist in the rain forest.

"What about Cesar and Heriberto?" Zoe took a guess. "Are they your brothers?"

"Yes." The young woman struggled with the gaping curtain.

Behind Tia's flailing arms, Zoe caught a glimpse of packing boxes, jumbled stock, mounds of trash. "You're moving out?"

"Thanks to you. We have to close shop just when business is good."

Zoe snorted. "I'm not at fault. Jag's illegal dealings are at fault. It wasn't only the lust potion, was it? You sold poisons and other concoctions beneath the counter, too."

The woman's lids dropped. Her lips tightened. "I don't know what you mean," she whispered, nearly drowned out by Tia's continuing diatribe.

Zoe felt a twinge of compassion. "Where will you go?"

"We have ways to disappear."

"Is that what happened to Jag and your brothers?" Ethan asked from behind Zoe.

The woman lifted her chin defiantly. "Tia says that she will curse you for a thousand years for taking Jag away."

Zoe recoiled. "*I* don't have Jag. Don't you know where he is?"

The young woman only shook her head, her face sad.

"Chac? Was it Chac who took him?"

The niece's eyes betrayed uncertainty and a glint of worry. "My *tia* believes that Chac was sent here by a Mayan medicine man. For retribution." She lowered her voice even more and Zoe had to lean forward to catch every word. "*Balam K'am-bi* was never meant to leave our people's village. The medicine man promised pain and suffering to those who disobeyed."

"But Jag didn't listen. He produced the potion here for a profit."

After a glance over her shoulder at the curtain that was no longer bulging, the niece shrugged. Her closed expression professed that she would say no more. From the back room, Tia's voice wailed.

"I'm not to blame," Zoe said. She turned and walked away.

Kathryn took Zoe's arm when she wavered on her boot heels as the old woman's screeching and moaning followed them even out to the sidewalk. Jag had dug his own grave, that was true. But she knew what Tia was suffering in losing a loved one.

"So THAT'S WHAT HAPPENED to Jag," Zoe said, slurping a strawberry milkshake through a straw.

Donovan watched her from behind his desk, thinking that if she came around any more often, they'd have to issue her a lab coat. With sequins and feathers and her name embroidered in sparkly thread. He used to think that she didn't fit into his life, that every time she came here, she was out of place. But he'd been wrong. Seeing her now, she looked right. Precisely, perfectly, indubitably right.

Zoe sat on a corner of his desk, oblivious, dangling her legs and knocking the heels of her lime-green boots. Except for her frown, she seemed to be back to normal since their Mojave experience. Although normal for Zoe was extraordinary for anyone else.

"Did you tell the police you'd talked to Jag's niece?" he asked.

"Nope. There's no need. I'm sure she and Tia have been questioned and the shop searched, since they were still open and doing business." She stirred the straw. "I don't want to cause them more trouble."

"Zoe."

"I know, I know. Jag was the culprit. But I suppose I do feel the tiniest bit guilty. It was me sticking my needle nose in and digging around that brought about what happened. So don't give me that play-it-by-the-book look—oh. You're *not* giving me that look. How come you're not giving me the look?"

"Because you're right. Justice has been served."

"Chac style." She shuddered. "It doesn't bear thinking of."

"You're assuming Jag was killed." Donovan walked around the desk, itching to get his hands on her even though he'd promised himself there'd be no more funny business anywhere near the lab. They had less privacy these days. His colleague had returned from her maternity leave, but luckily she was gone today, testifying in court.

Zoe put down the shake. "You think he wasn't?"

"Chac only said Jag would be taken care of. So maybe they stuck bamboo under his nails or strung him up or sentenced him to penance in the alligator swamp. We don't know." He slid his hands along her thighs and up to her hips. One tug and she was on the edge of the desk and wrapping her legs around him for balance.

She hooked a finger in the buttonhole of his lab coat. "You're only saying that to make me feel better."

"You don't feel better." He dropped his face near her neck and inhaled. He molded her buttocks. "You feel fine. So damn fine."

"Mmm. Ethan, my friend Ethan," she said and sighed as Donovan kissed her neck and licked behind her ear, "the one who's the crime reporter, uh, well, um, he's been following the poison cases and he says—"

Donovan nipped her bottom lip. "Yes?"

She touched the same spot with her tongue. Her eyes were bright and speculative. "He says that Jag was definitely selling poisons. Calling them Lover's Revenge and Black Widow, with the counterfeit versions on the shelves, the same way he sold the lust potion. Supposedly they weren't strong enough to be toxic, but obviously someone screwed *that* up, right?" She blinked at him. "I don't suppose you can tell me what the results were for various cases of suspected poisoning?"

He smiled. "Are you asking me to reveal confidential information?"

She punched him in the shoulder.

He caught her hands, becoming serious. "Zoe, honey, I'm walking a thin line as it is, with the dozens of rules I've broken over the lust potion. I know you want me to be more reckless, but I just can't. I'm not the guy I was in the Mojave."

She smiled at him. As if he was so wrong that she didn't even have to bother explaining.

"What about the lust potion?" she asked. "Is it okay if I publish the information you gave me, you know, about the jaguar pheromones?"

"Anonymous source?"

She made a zipping motion across her lips. "Of course."

He nodded. "There is another option." For a couple of seconds he debated with himself, the strict scientist fighting the lover's desire to please her above all else.

It was a struggle. But in the end, Zoe would always win out.

"You could have a sample analyzed commercially. That would give you full access to *all* the results."

"Great, except I don't have any, remember?"

"I have plenty of the freeze-dried sample remaining. Naturally, you can't touch that. But I never did dispose of the remaining liquid after I took that one gulp. It might show up in your pocket or in your fridge or in your purse. Who knows?"

She let out a yip of excitement and threw her arms around him. "Ah, Shane, I love you." She smacked big kisses across his face.

He was soaring. "I'll leave it up to you to decide what you want to do with the potion. Analyze it…"

"Or use it," she said, her eyes getting big at the prospect. "Oh, my goodness. What a quandary."

He kissed her. "Either way, I'm—"

The office door opened. Guillermo stood staring at them, his face going red. "Jeez, not again."

"Go find Mandy Rae," Donovan said, nuzzling Zoe's neck. He'd never get enough of her, with or without the potion.

"Sure, boss."

"Wait a sec, Gil." Zoe put a hand on Donovan's

chest to keep him at bay. "Are you and Mandy Rae still an item?"

"Uh, no." Gil made a face. "She acted all interested that one day, but ever since, I'm like nothing to her. Just a bother." His shoulders slumped. "I'm giving up."

"Excellent. I mean, I'm sorry she dropped you, but in that case, would you like to come to a Christmas party I'm giving next week? I have a friend I want you to meet."

"Heck, yeah. I'd love to be at one of your parties."

Zoe giggled. "You've heard about them?"

Gil nodded eagerly. "From Dr. Shane. He was always griping—uh, talking about your parties."

"Get out of here, Gil," Donovan said.

The intern grinned. "Sure, boss." He slammed the door with a decided flourish.

"About this party," Donovan said. "Am I invited?"

Zoe eyed him, pretending doubt. "Will you come this time?"

"With bells on."

She beamed. "That should be a sight."

"And about what you said a little while ago, concerning this Shane guy…"

"What did I say?"

"That you loved him."

"I do." She pulled off his glasses and kissed his eyes, his nose, his mouth. "I love you, Shane."

"Donovan."

"Yes, him too."

He held her face between his hands. "Say it."

"Oh, all right." Her eyes glittered with teary happiness. "I love you, Donovan…Shane."

He laughed. "Good enough. I love you, too, Zoe Aberdeen."

Epilogue

A WEEK LATER, ZOE'S PARTY was in full swing. She'd hung red pepper Christmas lights all around the apartment and decorated her brand-new eight-foot pink-glitter tree with a slapdash assortment of ornaments, from New Englandy sleigh bells and snowmen she'd pulled out of boxes saved from the Aberdeens' traditional holidays, to the bead garlands Donovan had brought home one day, to the paper cutouts of snowflakes and cardboard stars wrapped in foil that she and Hailey had been making all week. Salsa music alternated with Christmas carols. The buffet was a little bit of everything, including strange spicy concoctions of Zoe's and lutefisk from Birgitta, supplemented by an assortment of potluck dishes brought by the other guests.

The guests. Donovan had met only half of them before the party. They were as varied as everything else she did, including dishwashers and chefs out of the same restaurant, neighbors from every house on the block, coworkers like Gil—who'd hit it off with Hailey after an awkward beginning—plus Zoe's accountant, her hairdresser, wannabe-famous party girls and full-fledged famous athletes like the Olympic volleyball player who'd placed the star at the top of the tree.

But it was those closest to Zoe who had gathered around at her request. Kathryn Walters in blue silk, with Coyote Sullivan, the ex-sports editor who couldn't stop looking at her. The Brit, Ethan Ramsey, holding hands with Detective Nicole Arroyo, looking very nonofficial with loose hair and a deep red dress with bell sleeves and a neckline that displayed her voluptuous shape.

Zoe passed out small gifts, each wrapped in a different color, with bows that frothed with curls and corkscrews of ribbon. "These presents are special. Something just for us." There was one for Donovan and even one for herself. "I got them because we share a secret gift. I think you all can guess what I mean."

The group exchanged amused looks. They knew very well what they had in common.

"Go on," Zoe urged. "Open them."

Wrappings flew. Each opened a small jeweler's box. Kathryn breathed a soft, "Ooh," and lifted out a delicate chain. The charm dangling from it was a small platinum jaguar.

Nicole's necklace was identical. "Beautiful, Zoe. Thank you."

The men displayed their onyx jaguar tie tacks.

"Thanks, Zoe. I've always wanted to belong to a secret society," Coyote said with one of his devastating smiles.

"How much of a secret will it be once your story is published?" Ethan asked.

Zoe conceded with a laugh. "Not very. But now that Jag has been forcibly deported by Chac, I think no one will ever again experience the lust potion the way we did."

"How was that?" Donovan asked, even though he knew.

Zoe shined. "For us, *Balam K'am-bi* wasn't only about lust. We were the lucky few who also found true love."

* * * * *

Design Tip of the Day

Ambience is everything. Imagine eating a foie gras at a luncheonette counter or a side of coleslaw at Le Cirque. It's not a matter of food but one of atmosphere. Remember that when planning your dining room design.

—Tips from *Teddi.com*

"Now that's the kind of man you should be looking for," my mother, the self-appointed keeper of my shelf-life stamp, says. She points with her fork at a man in the corner of the Steak-Out Restaurant, a dive I've just been hired to redecorate. Making this restaurant look four-star will be hard, but not half as hard as getting through lunch without strangling the woman across the table from me. "*He* would make a good husband."

"Oh, you can tell that from across the room?" I ask, wondering how it is she can forget that when we had trouble getting rid of my last husband, she shot him. "Besides being ten minutes away from death if he actually eats all that steak, he's twenty years too old for me and—shallow woman that I am—twenty pounds too heavy. Besides, I am *so* not looking for another husband here. I'm looking to design a new image for this place, looking for some sense of ambience, some feeling, something I can build a proposal on for them."

My mother studies the man in the corner, tilting her head, the better to gauge his age, I suppose. I think she's grimacing, but with all the Botox and Restylane injected into that face, it's hard to tell. She takes another bite of her steak salad, chews slowly so that I don't miss the fact that the steak is a poor cut and tougher than it should be. "You're concentrating on the wrong kind of proposal," she says finally. "Just look at this place, Teddi. It's a dive. There are hardly any other diners. What does *that* tell you about the food?"

"That they cater to a dinner crowd and it's lunchtime," I tell her.

I don't know what I was thinking bringing her here with me. I suppose I thought it would be better than eating alone. There really are days when my common sense goes on vacation. Clearly, this is one of them. I mean, really, did I not resolve less than three weeks ago that I would not let my mother get to me anymore?

What good are New Year's resolutions, anyway?

Mario approaches the man's table and my mother studies him while they converse. Eventually Mario leaves the table with a huff, after which the diner glances up and meets my mother's gaze. I think she's smiling at him. That, or she's got indigestion. They size each other up.

I concentrate on making sketches in my notebook

and try to ignore the fact that my mother is flirting. At nearly seventy, she's developed an unhealthy interest in members of the opposite sex to whom she isn't married.

According to my father, who has broken the TMI rule and given me Too Much Information, she has no interest in sex with him. Better, I suppose, to be clued in on what they aren't doing in the bedroom than have to hear what they might be doing.

"He's not so old," my mother says, noticing that I have barely touched the Chinese chicken salad she warned me not to get. "He's got about as many years on you as you have on your little cop friend."

She does this to make me crazy. I know it, but it works all the same. "Drew Scoones is not my little 'friend.' He's a detective with whom I—"

"Screwed around," my mother says. I must look shocked, because my mother laughs at me and asks if I think she doesn't know the "lingo."

What I thought she didn't know was that Drew and I actually tangled in the sheets. And, since it's possible she's just fishing, I sidestep the issue and tell her that Drew is just a couple of years younger than me and that I don't need reminding. I dig into my salad with renewed vigor, determined to show my mother that Chinese chicken salad in a steak place was not the stupid choice it's proving to be.

After a few more minutes of my picking at the wilted leaves on my plate, the man my mother has me nearly engaged to pays his bill and heads past us toward the back of the restaurant. I watch my mother take in his shoes, his suit and the diamond pinkie ring that seems to be cutting off the circulation in his little finger.

"Such nice hands," she says after the man is out of sight. "Manicured." She and I both stare at my hands. I have two popped acrylics that are being held on at weird angles by bandages. My cuticles are ragged and there's marker decorating my right hand from measuring carelessly when I did a drawing for a customer.

Twenty minutes later she's disappointed that he managed to leave the restaurant without our noticing. He will join the list of the ones I let get away. I will hear about him twenty years from now when—according to my mother—my children will be grown and I will still be single, living pathetically alone with several dogs and cats.

After my ex, that sounds good to me.

The waitress tells us that our meal has been taken care of by the management and, after thanking Mario, the owner, complimenting him on the wonderful meal and assuring him that once I have redecorated his place people will be flocking here in droves (I actually use those words and ignore my mother when she rolls her eyes), my mother and I head for the restroom.

My father—unfortunately not with us today—has the patience of a saint. He got it over the years of living with my mother. She, perhaps as a result, figures he has the patience for both of them, and feels justified having none. For her, no rules apply, and a little thing like a picture of a man on the door to a public restroom is certainly no barrier to using the john. In all fairness, it does sccm silly to stand and wait for thc ladics' room if no one is using the men's room.

Still, it's the idea that rules don't apply to her, signs don't apply to her, conventions don't apply to her. She knocks on the door to the men's room. When no one answers she gestures to me to go in ahead. I tell her that I can certainly wait for the ladies' room to be free and she shrugs and goes in herself.

Not a minute later there is a bloodcurdling scream from behind the men's room door.

"Mom!" I yell. "Are you all right?"

Mario comes running over, the waitress on his heels. Two customers head our way while my mother continues to scream.

I try the door, but it is locked. I yell for her to open it and she fumbles with the knob. When she finally manages to unlock and open it, she is white behind her two streaks of blush, but she is on her feet and appears shaken but not stirred.

"What happened?" I ask her. So do Mario and the waitress and the few customers who have migrated to the back of the place.

She points toward the bathroom and I go in, thinking it serves her right for using the men's room. But I see nothing amiss.

She gestures toward the stall, and, like any self-respecting and suspicious woman, I poke the door open with one finger, expecting the worst.

What I find is worse than the worst.

The husband my mother picked out for me is sitting

on the toilet. His pants are puddled around his ankles, his hands are hanging at his sides. Pinned to his chest is some sort of Health Department certificate.

Oh, and there is a large, round, bloodless bullet hole between his eyes.

Four Nassau County police officers are securing the area, waiting for the detectives and crime scene personnel to show up. They are trying, though not very hard, to comfort my mother, who in another era would be considered to be suffering from the vapors. Less tactful in the twenty-first century, I'd say she was losing it. That is, if I didn't know her better, know she was milking it for everything it was worth.

My mother loves attention. As it begins to flag, she swoons and claims to feel faint. Despite four No Smoking signs, my mother insists it's all right for her to light up because, after all, she's in shock. Not to mention that signs, as we know, don't apply to her.

When asked not to smoke, she collapses mournfully in a chair and lets her head loll to the side, all without mussing her hair.

Eventually, the detectives show up to find the four patrolmen all circled around her, debating whether to administer CPR, smelling salts or simply call the paramedics. I, however, know just what will snap her to attention.

"Detective Scoones," I say loudly. My mother parts the sea of cops.

"We have to stop meeting like this," he says lightly

to me, but I can feel him checking me over with his eyes, making sure I'm all right while pretending not to care.

"What have you got in those pants?" my mother asks him, coming to her feet and staring at his crotch accusingly. "*Baydar?* Everywhere we Bayers are, you turn up. You don't expect me to buy that this is a coincidence, I hope."

Drew tells my mother that it's nice to see her, too, and asks if it's his fault that her daughter seems to attract disasters.

Charming to be made to feel like the bearer of a plague. He asks how I am.

"Just peachy," I tell him. "I seem to be making a habit of finding dead bodies, my mother is driving me crazy and the catering hall I booked two freakin' years ago for Dana's bat mitzvah has just been shut down by the Board of Health!"

"Glad to see your luck's finally changing," he says, giving me a quick squeeze around the shoulders before turning his attention to the patrolmen, asking what they've got, whether they've taken any statements, moved anything, all the sort of stuff you see on TV, without any of the drama. That is, if you don't count my mother's threats to faint every few minutes when she senses no one's paying attention to her.

Mario tells his waitstaff to bring everyone espresso, which I decline because I'm wired enough. Drew pulls him aside and a minute later I'm handed a cup of coffee that smells divinely of Kahlúa.

The man knows me well. Too well.

His partner, whom I've met once or twice, says he'll interview the kitchen staff. Drew asks Mario if he minds if he takes statements from the patrons first and gets to him and the waitstaff afterward.

"No, no," Mario tells him. "Do the patrons first." Drew raises his eyebrow at me like he wants to know if I get the double entendre. I try to look bored.

"What is it with you and murder victims?" he asks me when we sit down at a table in the corner.

I search them out so that I can see you again, I almost say, but I'm afraid it will sound desperate instead of sarcastic.

My mother, lighting up and daring him with a look to tell her not to, reminds him that *she* was the one to find the body.

Drew asks what happened *this time*. My mother tells him how the man in the john was "taken" with me, couldn't take his eyes off me and blatantly flirted with both of us. To his credit, Drew doesn't laugh, but his smirk is undeniable to the trained eye. And I've had my eye trained on him for nearly a year now.

"While he was noticing you," he asks me, "did *you* notice anything about him? Was he waiting for anyone? Watching for anything?"

I tell him that he didn't appear to be waiting or watching. That he made no phone calls, was fairly intent on eating and did, indeed, flirt with my mother. This last bit Drew takes with a grain of salt, which was the way it was intended.

"And he had a short conversation with Mario," I tell

him. "I think he might have been unhappy with the food, though he didn't send it back."

Drew asks what makes me think he was dissatisfied, and I tell him that the discussion seemed acrimonious and that Mario looked distressed when he left the table. Drew makes a note and says he'll look into it and asks about anyone else in the restaurant. Did I see anyone who didn't seem to belong, anyone who was watching the victim, anyone looking suspicious?

"Besides my mother?" I ask him, and Mom huffs and blows her cigarette smoke in my direction.

I tell him that there were several deliveries, the kitchen staff going in and out the back door to grab a smoke. He stops me and asks what I was doing checking out the back door of the restaurant.

Proudly—because, while he was off forgetting me, dropping by only once in a while to say hi to Jesse, my son, or drop something by for one of my daughters that he thought they might like, I was getting on with my life—I tell him that I'm decorating the place.

He looks genuinely impressed. "Commercial customers? That's great," he says. Okay, that's what he *ought* to say. What he actually says is "Whatever pays the bills."

"Howard Rosen, the famous restaurant critic, got her the job," my mother says. "You met him—the good-looking, distinguished gentleman with the *real* job, something to be proud of. I guess you've never read his reviews in *Newsday*."

Drew, without missing a beat, tells her that Howard's

reviews are on the top of his list, as soon as he learns how to read.

"I only meant—" my mother starts, but both of us assure her that we know just what she meant.

"So," Drew says. "Deliveries?"

I tell him that Mario would know better than I, but that I saw vegetables come in, maybe fish and linens.

"This is the second restaurant job Howard's got her," my mother tells Drew.

"At least she's getting *something* out of the relationship," he says.

"If he were here," my mother says, ignoring the insinuation, "he'd be comforting her instead of interrogating her. He'd be making sure we're both all right after such an ordeal."

"I'm sure he would," Drew agrees, then looks me in the eyes as if he's measuring my tolerance for shock. Quietly he adds, "But then maybe he doesn't know just what strong stuff your daughter's made of."

It's the closest thing to a tender moment I can expect from Drew Scoones. My mother breaks the spell. "She gets that from me," she says.

Both Drew and I take a minute, probably to pray that's all I inherited from her.

"I'm just trying to save you some time and effort," my mother tells him. "My money's on Howard."

Drew withers her with a look and mutters something that sounds suspiciously like "fool's gold." Then he excuses himself to go back to work.

I catch his sleeve and ask if it's all right for us to

leave. He says sure, he knows where we live. I say goodbye to Mario. I assure him that I will have some sketches for him in a few days, all the while hoping that this murder doesn't cancel his redecorating plans. I need the money desperately, the alternative being borrowing from my parents and being strangled by the strings.

My mother is strangely quiet all the way to her house. She doesn't tell me what a loser Drew Scoones is—despite his good looks—and how I was obviously drooling over him. She doesn't ask me where Howard is taking me tonight or warn me not to tell my father about what happened because he will worry about us both and no doubt insist we see our respective psychiatrists.

She fidgets nervously, opening and closing her purse over and over again.

"You okay?" I ask her. After all, she's just found a dead man on the toilet, and tough as she is that's got to be upsetting.

When she doesn't answer me I pull over to the side of the road.

"Mom?" She refuses to meet my eyes. "You want me to take you to see Dr. Cohen?"

She looks out the window as if she's just realized we're on Broadway in Woodmere. "Aren't we near Marvin's Jewelers?" she asks, pulling something out of her purse.

"What have you got, Mother?" I ask, prying open her fingers to find the murdered man's ring.

"It was on the sink," she says in answer to my dropped jaw. "I was going to get his name and address and have you return it to him so that he could ask you out. I thought it was a sign that the two of you were meant to be together."

"He's dead, Mom. You understand that, right?" I ask. You never can tell when my mother is fine and when she's in la-la land.

"Well, I didn't know that," she shouts at me. "Not at the time."

I ask why she didn't give it to Drew, realize that she wouldn't give Drew the time in a clock shop and add, "…or one of the other policemen?"

"For heaven's sake," she tells me. "The man is dead, Teddi, and I took his ring. How would that look?"

Before I can tell her it looks just the way it is, she pulls out a cigarette and threatens to light it.

"I mean, really," she says, shaking her head like it's my brains that are loose. "What does he need with it now?"

nocturne™

**WAS HE HER SAVIOR
OR HER NIGHTMARE?**

HAUNTED
LISA CHILDS

Years ago, Ariel and her sisters were separated for
their own protection. Now the man who vowed
revenge on her family has resumed the hunt, and
Ariel must warn her sisters before it's too late.
The closer she comes to finding them, the more
secretive her fiancé becomes. Can she trust the man
she plans to spend eternity with? Or has he been
waiting for the perfect moment to destroy her?

On sale December 2006.

SNHDEC

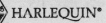

In February, expect MORE
from

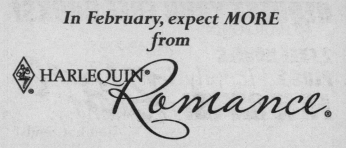

HARLEQUIN®
Romance®

as it increases to six titles per month.

What's to come...

Rancher and Protector

Part of the
Western Weddings
miniseries

BY JUDY CHRISTENBERRY

The Boss's
Pregnancy Proposal

BY RAYE MORGAN

Don't miss February's
incredible line up of authors!

www.eHarlequin.com   HRINCREASE

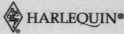

HARLEQUIN®

Blaze™

COMING NEXT MONTH

www.eHarlequin.com

HBCNM1206